TAKE COVER

A NOVELLA IN THE ECHO PLATOON SERIES

MARLISS MELTON

A NOTICE TO THE READER/LIMIT OF LIABILITY/DISCLAIMER OF WARRANTY:

James-York Press
Williamsburg, Virginia

Edited by Sydney J. Baily
Cover Design by Dar Dixon
Print Layout by BB eBooks

ISBN-13: 978-1-938732-25-6
ISBN-10: 1-938732-25-1

DEDICATION

This one is for you, Mike. Thank you for
resurrecting my faith in heroes.

ACKNOWLEDGEMENTS

An author has hit her stride when her readers join her in crafting a story. I am so blessed to have loyal fans who not only proofread my work but to help me come up with the words! Janie Hawkins, I loved having you back in my life. Please stay in it!

For all the members of my Special Reconnaissance Team who helped this time around—Hooyah! (If you are a huge fan and want to be a member, contact me on Facebook)

Still, even with so much help, I would be so, so bad without my best friend and editor,
Sydney J. Baily, to guide me.
God bless all y'all, as we say here in Virginia!

CHAPTER ONE

PIPED-IN SPANISH GUITAR music masked the sound of LT Mitchell Thoreau's footsteps as he crossed the tiled foyer of Hotel Leonardo, steps ahead of his two teammates. Having come straight from Barcelona International Airport, the three Navy SEALs intended to enjoy their vacation to its fullest. One look at the lovely lady working behind the reception counter, and Mitch lengthened his stride to get to her first. Being on vacation lent him confidence he didn't usually have with women.

"Hola," he said, putting his Spanish to good use and summoning what he hoped approximated a confident grin. "Tenemos una reservación."

The hotel employee looked up with a friendly smile. Amber brown eyes widened as they skimmed over him and then peered past him to encompass his approaching friends.

"Welcome to Barcelona," she said in flawless

English.

"You sound American." Mitch's gaze slid to her name tag—*Katrina Ferrer*. Her neat breasts, straining the fabric of a white button-up blouse, were perfect.

"My mother was from Kansas." She shrugged at the unlikelihood that her mother would be from a landlocked state nearly 5,000 miles away. "I think she took a hot-air balloon to get here. My father is Catalan, though, and I've lived here my whole life."

"So you speak English, Spanish, *and* Catalan," Mitch deduced just as Austin and Chuck stepped up beside him.

"Yes, I do." She sent all three of them a dazzling smile. "What name is your reservation under?"

"Thoreau." He'd inherited the name from his ancestor, Henry David Thoreau. However, since she'd probably never heard of the American novelist and philosopher, Mitch spelled his last name as she lifted slim hands to the keyboard. No wedding ring, he noticed.

"Good of you to visit Barcelona, given the state of things," she said, glancing up to gauge his reaction.

Mitch hummed in acknowledgement. Their week-long trip to Spain had been planned about a year earlier—well before Catalonia's push for independence had become a real issue. "Our flight was nonrefundable. We just came from the airport," he added.

"Thank you for coming all the same," Katrina insisted. "You could have stayed home."

"But then I would never have met you." It sounded like a pick-up line, but he was being perfectly honest.

Her fingers froze for one second—the only indication that she'd heard him. Then she clicked her mouse while staring at the screen. "Here you are. Just one room for the three of you?" She arched an eyebrow at him inquiringly.

At that moment, Mitch so wished he had a room to himself. Since he and his teammates were used to bunking in the same place and didn't plan to sleep much anyway, sharing a room had seemed like the smartest way to conserve money. "Unfortunately," he said, and he had to stop himself from waggling his eyebrows at her.

Her cheeks had taken on a pinkish hue. "And you're here for only two nights?"

"Our plans are flexible," he replied. For the chance to spend more time with her, he'd happily remain in Barcelona all week, though the plan was to continue to Seville and then to Madrid, spending three days in each of the cities.

Austin Collins put his elbows on the counter. "Are all the girls in Barcelona as pretty as you?" he asked her.

Mitch winced at the twenty-year-old's lack of subtlety.

Katrina merely smiled. "Of course." She glanced at Chuck Suzuki, as if expecting him to chime in, but Chuck rarely spoke, and when he did, he used metaphors—hence his call sign, Haiku.

Katrina laid a sheet in front of Mitch. "Here are our hotel policies. Let me get your signature on the credit card, and then you'll be all set."

He signed the slip with his boldest and best signature. "How do you feel about the Civil Guards?" he asked, putting the pen down.

Since arriving at the airport, he'd felt like the strong presence of the national police force smacked of foreign occupation—except that, of course, Catalonia was still a province of Spain. *La Guardia Civil* were everywhere, impossible not to notice in their blue ball caps and armed with assault rifles. He'd seen the clashes on the news between them and the citizens of Barcelona and wondered if Spain was going to turn into another Northern Ireland.

Tension tightened Katrina's sun-kissed face. "You understand what's going on?" she countered.

"Of course." The world was watching. Barcelona, the seat of Catalonia's government, had passed a vote declaring Catalonia an independent republic. In recent history, up to the point of Francisco Franco's dictatorship in 1939, Catalans had ruled themselves.

They enjoyed their own culture, their own language, and their cry for autonomy was being heard across the globe. Yet Spain could not afford to release them. Secession would cripple her economy as half the nation's wealth flowed from and through Catalonia's thriving ports.

"Things feel pretty tense out there," Mitch prompted, giving voice to his first impression, and wondering how she felt about it.

"It's not so bad." She shrugged again. "Madrid likes to pretend she controls us now, but we will have our way eventually—through peaceful resistance."

"Uh-huh." Mitch wasn't sure he believed her. Glancing around the quiet hotel lobby, he could only imagine how the unrest had affected the tourism industry.

"We are peace-loving people," Katrina added. "We don't believe in violence. If we did, we would have an army." She gestured outside as if that settled the matter.

"The will of the people should not be ignored." Haiku had finally spoken up.

Katrina's eyebrows pulled together as she considered him. "Well, that's true," she agreed. "But violence is not the answer."

Mitch could only hope she was right. His commander, Captain Montgomery, had given the three of them strict orders to carry their passports on their persons, and stay the hell out of trouble—good advice, since Austin loved to fight. The young SEAL's penchant for using his fists, paired with his love of the Flintstones, had given him his code name, Bam-Bam.

"Here are your three room keys."

As Katrina detailed some of the hotel's amenities, Mitch admired the way her lips moved when she talked. The golden hoops dangling from her earlobes drew his attention to the highlights in her incredibly long, honey-colored hair. He'd always liked long hair on a woman, and hers looked infinitely touchable.

"What do you plan to see while you're here?" She had asked all three of them, but she looked to Mitch for an answer.

"Um." With her eyes on him, it took a second to recall the sites he'd researched. "*La Sagrada Familia,*" he said, referring to the architect Antoni Gaudí's immense cathedral, still under construction a hundred years after his death. "The Gothic Quarter," he added, "and the Olympic Park."

She plucked several brochures from a stand on the counter and held them out. "Take these with you, then. They have coupons and general information. The one on top gives you a discount on one of the city bus tours. I highly recommend you do that. There's no better way to see the city. You can get off and on wherever you like."

Mitch took the opportunity to brush her fingers. Her gaze predictably jumped to his.

"You forgot to mention—" she paused to clear her throat—"*Las Ramblas*, which is a very famous street only one block from here."

If *Las Ramblas* hadn't been famous enough, the ISIS attack involving a van and several unfortunate pedestrians had placed it on the world's stage the past summer. That incident must have shaken her to the core having occurred so near the hotel.

"The most joyful street in the world," he said, seeking to obliterate the tragedy with a timeless literary allusion.

Her eyes flared in recognition. "You know Federico García Lorca?" she exclaimed, apparently delighted to hear the revolutionary poet quoted.

He shrugged in acknowledgment. "I'm a sucker for literature."

"Me, too." She studied him for a second. "I'm sorry to stare, but you have the bluest eyes I've ever seen."

Was she trying to flirt back? If so, it was working. Her frankness was far more seductive than the usual eyelash fluttering or lip pouting he'd learned to expect from women.

"I get that a lot," he admitted. This time, though,

his face heated, and he had to look away first.

"Well," she said, as an awkward pause fell between them.

Austin snorted in amusement, and Katrina fell back on her role as hotel employee.

"I hope you have a wonderful stay," she added brightly. "Can I get you any help with your luggage?" Seeing them with one large duffel bag apiece, she added, "No, I guess not."

"We travel light," Mitch explained.

Restricted by Spanish law from bringing their own firearms into the country, they probably carried more hand-held weapons in their bags than changes of clothing.

"Excellent. Be sure to let me know if I can do anything for you—if you need directions to places or suggestions for eating out. I'm sure I can help."

Mitch elbowed Austin to keep the kid from saying something inappropriate. "We will. Thank you, Katrina."

"Thank you, Katrina," Austin and Chuck chorused as they all turned and trooped to the elevator.

As the door closed softly behind them, taking Katrina out of view, Haiku murmured obliquely, "In the cherry blossoms' shade, there is no such thing as a stranger."

CHAPTER TWO

KATRINA SUFFERED A momentary letdown as the trio of riveting American men disappeared into the elevator. *Holy smokes.* Not to stereotype guests in general, but most Americans didn't look or act like those three. For one thing, they didn't have an ounce of extra body fat among them. Lean and muscular, they could have modeled athletic wear. And despite having come straight from the airport after an all-night flight, they looked ready to paint the town.

Mitchell Thoreau was especially bright eyed. "Stop it," she scolded herself, embarrassed by her comment to him. So his eyes were as blue as the Kansas sky that had astounded her every time her mother took her back to the States. And so what that he could quote Lorca? That didn't mean he was the man of her dreams. God knew when it came to men, her judgment wasn't the best anyway.

"Stop what?" Her father had apparently over-heard her as he pushed through the door leading from the lower level into the reception area.

"Nothing. Good morning, Pare," Katrina switched from English to Catalan, the language her father and brothers preferred. "Our three new guests just checked in," she informed him, relieving his worry that they might not show up. The vote for independence had taken quite a toll on their liveli-hood.

When her father didn't answer, Katrina turned to face him. Older than her mother had been by fifteen years, Felipe Ferrer had gone completely gray since his young wife's unexpected death five years earlier. Excess weight padded his previously trim mid-section. That morning, his preoccupied expression made him look especially haggard.

Guessing the reason for it, she cocked a hip against the counter and sighed. The Ferrer family had owned and operated Hotel Leonardo for three generations. Lately, her half-brothers, Martí and Jordi, had been so wrapped up in the political situation, they'd been slacking on their duties and forcing Katrina and her father to cover for them.

"Let me guess," she said as the phone began to ring. "Martí is making you cover his shift this morning."

"Yes." Without another word, Felipe reached

out to answer the telephone.

Katrina's resentment toward her brothers heated to a simmer. Did they have to be so concerned with the fate of Catalonia that they failed to look after their family? Their father, who had been widowed twice, was turning into a sad, old man. And what did they do? They ignored him to head up the Liberation Front, a group comprised of the same separatists who had goaded the Civil Guards in the last violent clash last month.

Katrina wished she could convince her brothers that their tactics were all wrong. Violence would only tighten Madrid's hold over Barcelona, fueling the fires on both sides until civil war became inevitable.

"I'm going to go talk to them."

Stuck on the phone with a client, her father shook his head frantically but couldn't stop her. Through the heavy door marked Employees Only and down to their basement quarters, Katrina hurried, whipping up her indignation as she went. At the same time, she cautioned herself to keep a level head. Martí and Jordi were older than she by a decade. What's more, Martí had a flash temper, and she would do well to watch her words if she hoped to persuade him that his obligation to family came first.

"I LIKE THAT saying about the cherry tree," Austin said as he tossed his duffel bag into the armoire in the corner of the room. "That Katrina chick is gorgeous."

"The metaphor was about hospitality, Bam-Bam," Mitch retorted, using Austin's code name to convey how young he was and how much he still had to learn. "Besides, she's too old for you," he added, claiming the luggage rack next to the bureau and leaving that for Chuck.

Chuck rose predictably to Austin's defense. "Everyone is the age of their heart," he insisted.

"Then she's still too old for him." Mitch unzipped his bag, hunting for his overnight kit and a fresh change of clothes. As the officer, he got first dibs on the shower. "You two want to plan where we're going first?" Finding what he needed, he headed for the bathroom.

"I say we hit up a bar," he heard Austin say.

"Oh, that's right, you're legal in this country." Mitch couldn't resist one last jibe. He slipped into the bathroom, dodging the dirty T-shirt Austin lobbed at him.

Seconds later, Mitch studied his naked reflection in the mirror wondering if Katrina had found him at all attractive. She'd made that comment about his eyes, but then lots of people did. Set in a face that was perfectly ordinary, his eyes were more of a liability than an asset in the places he and his teammates visited. He often had to wear brown contact lenses, or at least a dark pair of sunglasses to conceal them and a hat over his light-brown hair.

Apart from his startling eyes, not much set him apart from his superbly fit teammates. He was one inch taller than the average guy, and prone to keep quiet and let others talk. People tended not to notice him—at least when he hung around his swashbuckling, testosterone-driven teammates.

On top of that, he didn't have a specialty yet. After it was discovered he was a jack-of-all trades, he'd been sent to three different SEAL qualification courses, enabling him to step in as explosives expert, sniper, or medic. His competence made him popular, but only among his peers.

With women? Not so much. Women looked right through him. Part of that was his fault. He'd had priorities like finishing his education and making the Teams. When he became a SEAL, his teammates outshone him, rendering him nearly invisible. The only good news was, they were getting married, one by one, eliminating the competition.

My turn next, Mitch thought, and his mind went instantly to Katrina Ferrer. Why couldn't she be the one?

She lives in a different country, smart one.

Shaking his head at his ridiculous inner dialogue, Mitch turned and twisted on the shower faucet. Katrina Ferrer wasn't going to get involved with a guest who was planning to leave in two short days.

STORMING OUT OF the stairwell into their basement apartment, Katrina drew up short at the sound of Martí's voice raised in passionate defiance. Who was he talking to like that? Curious to find out, she hurried down the corridor and was amazed to hear other voices—several of them—murmuring in concurrence of what Martí was saying.

"...a statement they will understand," she heard him rant. "History teaches us this lesson—that progress has *never* come from peace."

Rounding the corridor, she blinked in astonishment as she ran into a gathering of ten or twelve people standing in their living area. Lack of available seating kept them on their feet. Over their heads, Katrina could see Martí, up on a chair, warming to his role as their spokesman.

"A new nation has never risen without strife," he insisted, gesturing with a bony hand. "And strife requires bloodshed. If we are to rise from the ashes then there has to be a fire first."

Several of his friends applauded. Katrina recognized them as radical-leaning ne'er-do-wells, men who'd milled around the neighborhood doing little to improve their circumstances.

Standing on tiptoe, she searched for her other brother Jordi, hoping to appeal to him to put a stop to this. Martí took sudden notice of her.

"You know the plan," he added, curtailing his speech abruptly. "Go but tell no one, or you will forever be known as a traitor."

"*Desperta Ferro!*"

The room reverberated with the rally cry—one Martí had borrowed from history and apparently popularized with this group of misfits. With a pinch of concern, Katrina considered what the words meant—awaken the iron. It occurred to her Martí was encouraging his little group of ragtag followers to fight physically for their independence.

Oh, my God, she thought, as they brushed past her to funnel out of the basement through an exit used exclusively by her family. Spying snacks laid out on their table, she turned to see what Martí had pilfered from the kitchen.

Her resentment rose. There wasn't money in this week's budget to replace the churros he had laid out, not with the tourist season being as dismal as this one. With jerky movements, she began to tidy up, combining the leftovers into a box.

"What are you doing down here?" The question, had it been a whip, would have flayed her with how harshly it was spoken.

Turning, Katrina found Martí and one loitering guest standing behind her, their expressions hostile.

"This is my home," she answered levelly. "I wasn't aware that I was forbidden from it."

Older than she by twelve years, Martí's sour disposition had carved deep grooves on either side of his thin lips. "Only pure Catalans may attend my meetings," he stated, sharing a superior look with his friend.

Katrina had accepted Martí's dislike of her. She obviously reminded him of her mother, Laura, a woman who'd captured Felipe's heart so soon after the death of Martí's own mother, that Martí had never viewed Laura as anything but the *other* woman. After Laura's death, Martí had transferred his resentment to Katrina. Jordi, at least, had been kinder to her.

Katrina pointed to the churros. "These are not to be given away for free," she stated. "They come at a cost, right out of our pockets."

"All things come at a cost," he surprised her by agreeing.

As he and his friend smirked simultaneously, she recalled his words about strife and fire. "I hope you're not planning to tangle with the *Benemérita*," she cautioned.

"*Benemérita*?" He scoffed at her use of the respectful term for the Spanish Civil Guard. "*La Guardia Civil* have no jurisdiction here. We have declared ourselves an independent republic. Therefore, they are nothing but foreign oppressors. We owe them *no* respect."

Katrina's concern deepened. She stepped closer, placing a hand on his arm to reason with him. "Your way of thinking is dangerous, Martí. Violence is never the solution."

"Don't talk to me." He shook off her touch. "You're not even one of us."

His condescension stung. Being half-American, she could never be fully Catalan—that was true. But she'd lived her whole life in northeast Spain, surrounded by the Catalan language and culture. Barcelona was her home.

"What are you planning?" she demanded, ignoring his taunt.

"It's none of your concern." Throwing an arm around his companion, he turned away with that man, murmuring directions under his breath.

Katrina wondered where Jordi, her more level-headed brother, was. Apparently, he hadn't attended this little rally. Perhaps he hadn't been invited.

Boxing the remaining churros, she carried them out of the *sala* to return them to the kitchen. When she handed the box to cook, that woman rolled her eyes and flung the box into the trash. Hotel Leonardo served only one meal a day in the small café. Cook clearly took pride in her fresh breakfast pastries.

A premonition of something terrible churned in Katrina as she returned to the lobby. She had caught wind of a dark plan—something involving strife and fire, ashes and revenge. What, exactly, was Martí and his small band of malcontents intending? Did he really think he could teach Madrid a lesson without landing himself in jail?

She needed to discover what her brother had in mind. Perhaps his rhetoric was just that, and his plans weren't as dire as her gut was insisting. Jordi would know. If he refused to tell her, she would threaten to expose his indiscretion with the cleaning woman to his wife.

One thing she would not do was discuss the matter with her father, whom she found still on the phone. Taking in his defeated posture and subdued voice, she kept her concerns to herself. Felipe was no doubt well aware of his sons' radical leanings. Yet he lacked both the energy and the resolve to stop them. To some extent, he likely even sympathized.

Katrina swallowed uneasily. She had just reassured their American guests that the Catalans were peaceable people. What if Martí went through with whatever act of violence he was planning and innocent people died or were hurt in the process?

He'd be no different than the ISIS extremist who'd run down tourists and locals alike on *Las Ramblas* last summer.

My God, what was the world coming to?

CHAPTER THREE

"LORDY, MY FEET hurt," Austin griped, propping his smart-looking cowboy boots on the cross bar at the base of Mitch's stool.

Across the pub table, Mitch shot Chuck a dry look. They had both told Austin before leaving the hotel to wear his sneakers as they were going to walk all afternoon throughout the city, exploring every nook and cranny before taking refuge in a cool, dark tavern. As it was only eight, they would drink a couple of beers at the bar first, then move to a table for dinner, resting their feet before dancing the night away.

"The only source of knowledge is experience," Chuck murmured.

"Who said that?" Austin challenged him.

"Albert Einstein."

"You can't argue with Albert," Mitch chimed in.

A wedge of evening sunlight entered through the

establishment's front door, and all three SEALs looked up from the bar to see who was coming in.

Austin recognized her first. "Hey, isn't that the receptionist at our hotel?"

Mitch straightened on his stool. Pleasure shot through him at the sight Katrina made, haloed by the sun's gold rays as she stood in the open door a minute searching the restaurant area. She wore the same white blouse she had worn at the front desk that morning. It was obvious she had come straight from the hotel to meet someone.

Loath to have her turn and walk out, Mitch stepped off his stool. "I'm going to go say hi." As he started out in her direction, Katrina caught sight of whomever she was looking for and struck out in their direction, disappearing behind a partition separating the bar from the dining area.

Mitch moved to where he could see her again, then froze to find her standing, arms akimbo, over a table littered with empty beer bottles and occupied by four men. One in particular, stocky and several years older than she, returned her disapproving glare with a belligerent expression.

Damn, she has a boyfriend, was the first thought that flitted through Mitch's brain, *and she just caught him out drinking with his friends.*

Well, of course she would have a boyfriend, as gorgeous as she was. On the other hand, he consoled himself, their break up looked imminent.

Keeping himself tucked out of sight, he waited to see what happened next. Katrina's tense voice reached his ears. She was issuing a request in Catalan. When three men scraped back their chairs and left the table, it was obvious she'd asked for a moment alone with her boyfriend. As they sauntered to the bar, Mitch pretended to tie his shoelace.

An urgent conversation reached his ears. Uttered in rapid Catalan, he could make no sense of it. The man whom Katrina addressed as Jordi refused to answer her pointed questions. It sounded like she threatened him. He thumped his hand on the table, causing Mitch to straighten in the event he needed to intervene.

He peeked back at the bar, where Jordi's three companions were ordering more drinks, taking no notice of the Americans. Hearing Jordi mutter something in a growl, Mitch eased out of hiding and slipped into a chair unnoticed.

Katrina stared at Jordi with an expression of horror. The pallor in her face wasn't simply a product of the pendant light hanging over their table.

She hissed something at the man across from her. Jordi then shoved his chair back, violently, causing Mitch to slide a hand into his pocket reaching for his spring-loaded, folding dagger as Jordi shot to his feet.

"Calla!" he shouted, which Mitch recognized as *shut up*.

Mitch was about to spring out of his own chair and cross the room to dissuade the boyfriend from further outbursts when the man tossed down a wad of euros and left the table. Passing Mitch, he skewered him with a suspicious glare, then made his way toward the door, gesturing with an impatient wave for his friends to follow him.

Looking back at Katrina, Mitch found her staring at him with her mouth hanging open.

She did not look happy to see him. Summoning his courage, he released the dagger in his pocket and crossed to where she sat.

"Where did you come from?" The way she switched so effortlessly from Catalan to English impressed him.

"I was sitting at the bar with my friends. We saw you come in." He glanced back at the door just as Jordi's friends were leaving. "Everything okay between you and…that guy?"

A crease appeared on her smooth forehead. "My brother," she said. "Half-brother, actually. We had different mothers."

Their familial relationship cheered Mitch immensely.

She, on the other hand, looked devastated as she dropped her gaze to the table.

"Sounded like you were arguing," he gently pressed.

She drew a deep breath as she lifted her eyes. "It's not something you want to hear," she said, politely telling him to butt out of her business.

He nodded with acceptance. "Would you care to join us for a drink since you're already here? Then maybe dinner after?"

Pulling out her cellphone, she glanced at the time. "Sure. I could use a drink right now."

Whatever her reasoning, he was just happy for the company. "Great. We're at the bar." Subduing a grin to a mere smile, he pulled her chair back. Then, with a light hand on her sleeve, he steered her around the partition back to the bar, where Chuck and Austin sat waiting. They both came to their feet, looking impressed at his accomplishment.

"Katrina, this is Chuck," Mitch said, making proper introductions.

Haiku ignored her proffered hand and bowed to her Japanese-style.

"And this is Bam-Bam," he added, ribbing the kid by using his pet name.

"Austin," Bam-Bam corrected him, pumping Katrina's hand over-enthusiastically.

"Nice to meet you, Austin."

Mitch swiped a seat from the empty table and set it behind Katrina's sweetly shaped bottom, right next to his stool. As she perched herself on it, he caught a whiff of her perfume, something sweet, yet bright and sensuous. It made him want to put his nose to her neck.

He put a hand lightly on her shoulder. "What can I get you from the bar?"

She tipped her head back to look at him. "I'll take a dry martini," she said, adding the type of gin she preferred, "and three olives, please."

"You got it."

Whatever she and her brother had discussed, it had clearly rattled her. With his teammates engaging her in conversation, Mitch stepped toward the bartender to relay her order. He made up his mind right then and there, he was going to divert Katrina from whatever unpleasantness had just ensued and give her something good to think about.

CHAPTER FOUR

KATRINA LAUGHED SO hard tears squeezed out the corners of her eyes and slid down her cheeks. Being this drunk was a little frightening. If not for the secure arms on either side escorting her along one of the many crooked side-streets splintering off *Las Ramblas*, she would have fallen on the paving stones. Mercifully, it was Saturday night and Sunday was her one day off each week. She suspected in a few hours, she would rue her over-indulgence. Then again, what might have been the worst night of her life was proving highly entertaining.

Mitchell Thoreau and his two friends had just about succeeded in helping her forget what Jordi had confessed earlier that evening. Even in her present state of hilarity, though, the memory of it had the power to sober her. It lay against her conscience like the sharp edge of a razor pressed against her jugular. She couldn't afford to ignore it much longer, but for the next hour or two, she would do her best.

Joining her fellow carousers in a song she didn't know, she led them toward the only dance club that stayed open until dawn. Since breaking up with Armando, Katrina had ceased to visit Razzmatazz. But what better time to make an appearance, should Armando be there, than in the company of not one but three virile men?

As they waded into the crush of humanity, ears assaulted by throbbing techno music, Katrina's gaze went straight to the head of coal-black hair on the dance floor. Armando gyrated against the lush curves of a brunette. The betrayal to which he'd subjected Katrina the year before scarcely stung. With relief, she grabbed Mitch Thoreau's hand and tugged him toward the dancers. Of her three new acquaintances, she felt powerfully drawn to him, like she'd known him all her life.

To her delight, he moved with subdued grace and perfect rhythm. Pinning his laser-blue eyes on her person, he watched her as she danced. A suggestion of a smile hovered on his handsome, ruddy lips. From the corner of her eye, she saw Armando do a double-take as he caught sight of them. Glimpsing jealousy in his expression, she proceeded to give her ex-lover something to regret and executed a move that would have made Beyoncé jealous—if the floor hadn't suddenly tipped.

Feeling herself fall, Katrina braced herself for humiliation, only to feel herself snatched upright again. Mitch set her back on her feet, only this time she was in his arms, properly subdued, and suddenly, pleasantly aware of how solid and strong he was.

"Okay, there?" He managed to sound concerned even while there was laughter in his voice.

"Fine." She felt her face grow hot.

He regarded her a moment. "You sure?"

An unexpected wave of nausea rolled through her. "Actually, I think I might throw up," she amended.

"Let's go sit down."

Supporting her as they went, Mitch helped her off the dance floor and away from the deafening music to the corner of the club. His friends had managed to secure a table there. Chuck guarded their camp while Austin cruised the dance floor's perimeter looking for potential dance partners.

As Katrina went to climb onto a stool, Mitch spanned her waist and set her effortlessly atop it. He pushed a full glass of water into her hands. "Time to hydrate," he suggested.

Touched by his thoughtfulness and a little bemused by his manhandling, Katrina stopped thinking of Armando and regarded Mitch over the top of her glass before taking a long drink. Until they'd touched shoulder to thigh minutes ago, she had never considered getting involved with a guest in her hotel. Having felt an unmistakable spark—one that was still warming her insides—she wondered if she ought to let her hair down a little and enjoy herself while she could.

"I almost made a fool of myself," she admitted, lowering her glass.

"My fault." His blue eyes seemed to burn through the shadows as he considered her. "Shouldn't have let you drink so much."

She quirked an eyebrow at him. "You think that's up to you?"

Her feisty question made his mouth twitch. "Apparently not. The least I can do is catch you when you fall." He glanced toward Armando, who had left the dance floor himself and was brooding at the bar. "Old flame?" Mitch guessed.

His astuteness surprised Katrina. "Yes," she admitted, hearing bitterness in her voice. She had let her rose-tinted glasses blind her to Armando's philandering nature.

Mitch, still standing, moved closer. His thigh brushed her knee, heightening her awareness of him. The scent of sports soap teased her nostrils.

He sent her a crooked smile. "What's his name?"

"Armando." She couldn't recall what she'd ever

seen in him.

"Don't look now but he's watching us."

The intel made her pulse quicken.

"Want to make him jealous?"

His smile widened to a grin, making him suddenly, unbearably appealing.

Thoughts of Armando could not have been farther from her mind. "Honestly, I don't care what he thinks," she retorted with a toss of her head.

Mitch caught her chin with warm fingers, bent at the waist and brushed his lips lightly, over hers, causing Katrina's eyes to widen in surprise. When he straightened again, she searched his expression with puzzlement. "Did *you* want to make him jealous?" she asked.

Mitch shrugged. "Not really. I just wanted kiss you."

"Oh." Well, that was different. His words stoked the warmth inside of her, turning it into a bonfire. "I'm sorry, but that kiss happened so fast I think I missed it."

He chuckled at her assertion. "That right? You need me to repeat it?"

"Yes, please," she said, aware that all the liquor she'd imbibed had made her bolder than usual.

Lifting her chin again, he lowered his head slowly, drawing his actions out with exaggerated care. "Pay attention this time," he whispered.

Every neuron in her brain was focused on the glide of his thumb as he brushed it across her lower lip. Her breath caught. His digit slid to her chin and gently depressed it. As her lips parted, he dipped his head and fastened his lips to hers. His tongue stroked through the opening he'd created. What resulted was a wave of lust as their mouths merged.

Tightening her hold to keep from keeling over, Katrina clung to Mitch and kissed him back. Not one sliver of awkwardness or doubt pricked her—only wonder and a sense of belonging. Their breaths tangled as they sucked in oxygen to fuel their fast-beating hearts, but neither one of them could seem to stop.

A sudden thought burst Katrina's bubble of contentment. He and his friends were not from Barcelona, nor even from Spain. Mitch would be leaving soon.

With an audible groan, Mitch tore his lips from hers.

"Damn," he muttered, his expression pained.

Something deep within her clutched as she realized he'd been thinking the very thing she had.

"You're beautiful," he said on a note of lament.

Her heart gave a pang. "Thank you."

"I wish—" He cut himself off and shook his head.

"You wish we'd met under different circumstances?" She hoped she was reading him right.

He nodded with feeling. "Yeah. That pretty much sums it up."

Pleased to discover her feelings weren't one-sided she added, "I want you to know I don't usually behave this way." The first rays of sobriety were casting light onto her inebriation, *and* her behavior. She didn't want him thinking she made a habit of kissing the guests who came to her hotel.

"I know." He traced the rise and fall of her knuckles.

His touch enthralled her. She desired nothing more than to be alone with him.

"Your brother upset you today," he commented.

The reminder of what Jordi had told her wrested Katrina from her pleasant thoughts. She had to avert her face to keep Mitch from glimpsing her suddenly stricken expression. Filling her lungs with the smell of reality—of sweaty bodies and stale, spilled beer—she let the horror of what Martí intended overshadow her present contentment.

"I'm sorry. I have to go home now." She slipped abruptly off the stool only to find her progress halted as a large hand encircled her wrist.

Without exerting an ounce of force, Mitch's grip conveyed resolve.

"I'll take you," he offered.

Seeing his two companions, Chuck and Austin,

dancing with a pair of brunettes, she shook her head. "No, no. Have fun with your friends. I can find my way back."

With an admonishing look, he transferred his hand to her elbow and steered her toward the exit, at the same time emitting a sharp whistle that rang in her ears and garnered his friends' attention. As they looked over, Mitch gestured with his head that he was leaving.

Katrina's face heated as everyone in the vicinity also took notice—including Armando, who scowled over his beer bottle. In light of her and Mitch's public kiss, who wouldn't assume they were hurrying out of the club so they could sleep together?

It doesn't matter what Armando thinks. At the same time a voice in Katrina's head murmured, "*Why not do it, if everyone thinks you did?*"

Glancing at Mitch as he held the heavy door for her, her knees seemed to melt as she considered his raw masculinity. Her heart began to beat erratically. A cool breeze played with her hair, heightening her feminine awareness. When Mitch caught up her hand in his, all she could think of was how slight she felt walking next to him, how safely protected. She realized he was walking toward Hotel Leonardo without her instruction, proving he'd retained some sense of where they were.

"You're safe with me, you know."

His words confirmed what she had sensed from their first meeting—Here was a gentleman, a *cavaller*. The real question was whether he was safe with her, uninhibited as she was.

The impulse, so out of character, to fall into bed with a man she scarcely knew ought to shock her into shamefullness. Yet, she couldn't shake the feeling that she'd known him all her life. Moreover, the thought of him leaving Barcelona in two short days left her grappling with desperation, as if she had to make a choice now or forever regret letting something rare and beautiful slip through her fingers.

Or was that her only motivation for wanting to sleep with him?

The memory of Marti's intent ripped though her thoughts. She would do just about anything to forget what she'd heard—including sleeping with a man she hardly knew.

CHAPTER FIVE

MITCH COULD TELL Katrina was sobering. So long as her hand was in his, she could walk in a straight line. In the quiet that fell between them, their footfalls echoed off the paving stones as they progressed through the labyrinth of narrow streets leading back to the hotel. Whatever had been troubling her about her interaction with her half-brother had evidently returned to weigh on her. He wished she'd tell him what it was, so he could help put it into perspective.

"I've never had a one-night stand," she stated out of the blue.

The comment, so at odds with what he'd thought she was thinking, pulled Mitch to a stop. A gas lamp mounted by an old paneled door found reflection in Katrina's long hair and put twin flames in her eyes as she lifted them inquiringly.

"Is that where this is heading?" He'd never had a

woman proposition him before.

"Maybe," she said, but it sounded more like a question than an answer.

While Mitch was certain sex with her would top any experience he'd ever had, only a schmuck took advantage of a woman who'd had too much to drink.

"I'm sorry, Katrina, but it wouldn't be right for me to sleep with you," he said with regret. But God knew he was tempted.

"Because I'm drunk?" she asked, heaving a sigh he found to be adorable.

"That's one reason."

"Because you're leaving soon?" she asked again.

"That's the other."

Before he went and changed his mind, Mitch squeezed her hand and continued up the narrow street. Katrina fell into step beside him, notably silent.

They hadn't walked ten feet when raucous laughter stormed up the alley behind them. A glance behind them showed three men hurrying to overtake them. The flare of a cigarette lit the face of Katrina's old flame.

Armando sneered back at him, making it evident he was coming after Mitch, and he'd brought along reinforcements.

Realizing who was following them, Katrina gave

a sound of disgust then directed a stream of Catalan over her shoulder. It didn't take much imagination to figure out what she was telling Armando.

All the same, that man responded in English for Mitch's benefit. "Oh, you want me to go home? But then I wouldn't get to knock out your friend's teeth."

His companions snickered at his clever comeback.

Katrina's grip tightened. "I'm serious, Armando. Leave us alone."

"Why, so you can fuck an American rather than have sex with your own boyfriend?"

"You're *not* my boyfriend," she growled in disgust.

Mitch heard little beyond the man's utter lack of respect. Sparing a thought for his folding dagger and backup blade, he decided he was better off using his hands so he didn't incite his CO's wrath by inadvertently killing a local.

Katrina must have felt him tensing. "Please ignore him. Let's just go." She tried tugging him away from the trio.

He backed her toward the nearest wall. "I'm sorry, honey. I can't let that pass. Stay right here. I can handle this," he assured her.

"But there are three of them," she cried in a frightened voice.

"I'll be fine." Squeezing her shoulders, he turned and walked toward his opponents.

Armando was all bravado as he tossed down his cigarette and swaggered up to Mitch. His two friends flanked him.

With no expectation of pacifying any one of them, Mitch noted each man's stance and position, confident he could eliminate all three in short order—providing Katrina didn't involve herself.

"American dog," Armando spat. Balling up his fist, he started to pull his arm back when a familiar voice echoed up the alley.

"Hey, losers."

Armando hesitated. Mitch groaned as Austin and Haiku materialized out of nowhere. Austin's grin was like a jag of lightning. He closed in, rubbing his hands with gleeful anticipation while Haiku drifted in his shadow, almost invisible.

"Let's even the odds, shall we?" Austin suggested.

Picturing the bloody aftermath and the ass-chewing he would get when news of the carnage reached Captain Montgomery's ears, Mitch offered Armando an alternative. "Or you could just walk away." Stepping aside, he gestured broadly to the empty street behind him.

In that precise second, two paramilitary members of the *Guardia Civil* rounded the street corner cradling their semi-automatics. Mitch's concern rose exponentially. Suddenly, he had more than his CO's reprimand to worry about. The guards' steps slowed as they took in the belligerent stances of the late-night revelers they'd run into.

The presence of the guards convinced Armando to accept Mitch's offer. With slouched shoulders and a muttered exchange, he and his friends hurried away, turning left at the intersection to avoid the *Guardia Civil* who remained on the opposite corner watching them go then turned their attention predictably to Mitch and company.

With Hotel Leonardo standing just beyond the guards, the foursome had no choice but to walk past them. Mitch's civil greeting prompted a barked command, uttered too swiftly for him to understand.

Katrina responded with a word of compliance.

"What'd he say?" he asked once the guards were out of earshot.

"He said it's past curfew," she replied.

"There's a curfew?"

"I guess there is now." The tension in her voice made her sound perfectly sober. "There must have been a skirmish somewhere. I was afraid this would happen."

Well, hell, Mitch thought. The fragile peace in Barcelona was starting to disintegrate. Maybe he and his friends ought to skip town and head to Seville two days early.

He thought about Katrina and immediately dismissed the idea.

As they neared the hotel's whitewashed walls and wrought-iron balconies, he recalled her round-about proposition: *I've never had a one-night stand.*

Given her tense expression as she led them to the double-wide door and unlocked it with a card from her pocket, Mitch guessed the aberrant act was now out of the question. Between their run-in with Armando and the news that a curfew had been declared, she may have already forgotten their deep and sudden connection.

Taking the door from her, he ushered everyone inside. In the dimly lit foyer that smelled of dried flowers, he caught up to Katrina, catching her arm before she got away from him.

As she turned to look at him, he called to his buddies, who proceeded to the elevator. "Hey, I'll be right up." Then he looked back at Katrina. "Can I see you tomorrow?" Despite how strangely the night had turned out, he yearned to spend more time with her.

She broke eye contact and wet her lips as if thinking.

"Can I take you on a date?" he clarified.

She drew a breath, touching a distracted hand to her forehead.

Had she forgotten she was willing to sleep with him just minutes ago?

"You said you had the day off," he reminded her. "I'm busy all morning with tours we scheduled, but I'm free at like five o'clock."

"Five o'clock? Okay," she finally said.

"Okay?" He wondered at her sudden profound distraction. Was Armando's taunt bothering her? The news of a curfew instated by Madrid?

"Yes, a date would be nice." She mustered a convincing smile for him, but all he read in her golden-brown eyes was concern.

"Meet you here in the lobby at five, then."

Katrina nodded and said nothing more.

Wanting to remind her of their connection, Mitch bent and brushed a lingering kiss across her cheek. He was pleased to feel her response as she leaned into him. "Thanks for taking us around. I'll see you here tomorrow."

The silky texture of her skin under his lips made it hard to walk away. But he could tell she needed time alone—to ponder what?

Frustration pricked him. The only thing he could do in the limited time left to them was to show Katrina how real men treated their women. That way, she would never forget him, just as he was certain he would never forget her.

CHAPTER SIX

"**G**UYS, I'VE GOT to head back to the hotel for my date." Glancing at his watch while seated on the upper floor of a moving double-decker, Mitch discovered that time had run away on him. Their trip to the Olympic Park, followed by lunch and a tour of *La Sagrada Familia*, had taken them late into the afternoon.

Haiku glanced at the map on his sat phone. Being the task unit's chief communications officer, he could access data anywhere in the world—at least when a U.S.-owned satellite was orbiting overhead. Mitch's iPhone, on the other hand, was useless whenever he went overseas.

"Get off at the next stop and walk north two blocks," Haiku advised.

Austin, who was plugged into his music, looked over in time to see Mitch slide to the edge of his seat. "Get some for me, brother," he called.

Mitch rolled his eyes. As the bus approached *Avinguda Diagonal*, he reminded Chuck about the newly instated curfew. Madrid had decreed that not a single soul should be walking the streets of Barcelona after three in the morning. Chuck acknowledged the reminder with a nod. The bus drew to a stop, and Mitch clambered off, hurrying in the direction of the hotel.

As he crossed the lobby, Katrina's father, a careworn gentleman who'd taken the time that morning to answer their last-minute transportation questions, glanced up. Mitch's respectful greeting went ignored. The man didn't even seem to recognize him from earlier.

It occurred to Mitch that the tension in the streets was equally evident within the Ferrer family. The number of *Guardia Civil* in Barcelona seemed to have tripled overnight. Regardless of what sights Mitch and his companions had toured that day, there were paramilitary policemen everywhere, casing the streets, shooting suspicious looks at the locals.

Clearly, the guards were there to discourage acts of rebellion, but considering how much and for how many decades Catalans had desired their independence, Mitch figured it was only a matter of time before tensions turned into violence.

Still pondering Spain's future, he showered and

shaved in record time before donning a lightweight blue button-up, tan slacks, and boat shoes. The previous night's near brush with violence reminded him to transfer his folding dagger from his jeans into the pocket of his slacks. The holster for his backup knife went around his left ankle, out of sight.

With a bounce in his step, Mitch left his room and headed for the lobby, arriving two minutes early.

Katrina was waiting by the check-in counter. Caught up in earnest conversation with her father, she failed to notice his approach. He sure as hell noticed her.

A black swing dress fell from her shoulders to the top half of her thighs, leaving most of her trim, golden legs bare. Her hair was caught up in a pony-tail, drawing his attention to her slender neck and the smooth skin peeking through the embroidery at the back of her dress. Strappy black heels encased her dainty feet. If he could have gotten away with picking her up and carrying her to his room right then, he might have tried it.

Felipe caught sight of him first, directing Katrina's attention over her shoulder. As she turned around, a convincing smile supplanted her agitated expression.

More family trouble, Mitch thought.

"Hello," he said, wishing he'd brought a flower for her hair as he bent to brush her cheek. Her perfume, he decided, would have made the flower redundant. "You look amazing."

She took in his neat attire. "So do you."

Pleased, Mitch cast a respectful nod at her father. "I'll take good care of her, sir," he promised, but that man was already turning away, mumbling to himself.

"Ready?" Mitch asked Katrina.

With a game smile and a familiarity that warmed him, she linked her arm with his. "Let's go," she said, drawing him toward the exit.

"You feel okay today?" he asked. Her fresh complexion and sexy eye makeup betrayed scant evidence of their late outing the night before. "No hangover?"

"No, I'm fine. You?" she asked, as he opened the door for her.

"I couldn't be better."

"Great." They stood on the stoop of the hotel grinning at each other. "Where are we going?" she prompted.

"I was hoping you could make that decision for me." Filaments of sunlight slanted across the street, bathing the townhouses across the street in gold. "Where's a good restaurant that's close to here?"

"Hmm." She turned her head predictably toward *Las Ramblas*, and her smile disappeared. "Let's go this way," she said, nodding in the opposite direction—one he'd never taken before.

Maybe she was remembering Armando and the crude words he'd spoken. Recalling his decision to eradicate that man's memory from her mind, Mitch steered Katrina toward the inner part of the sidewalk, taking the curb side in the event of a runaway car.

She glanced at him sidelong, looking at first bemused and then touched. A small smile lifted at the corners of her pink-glossed lips.

He had a hunch he'd be kissing that gloss off her long before their date was over.

"HOW'S THE GAZPACHO?"

Mitch's question, paired with his searching blue gaze, let Katrina know she wasn't doing so great a job of concealing her anxiety. They sat at an outdoor café she had visited many times before, *La Granja*, sheltered from the glare of the setting sun by a green awning. Mitch had ordered several different *tapas*, or light plates for them to share, including *jamón serrano* and *tortilla Española*. She herself had scarcely touched her chilled gazpacho, preferring to sip the sangria she'd ordered in the hopes that it would settle her nerves.

"It's good," she assured him, regretting their circumstances. If not for the weight of the world on her shoulders, she could well be enjoying the best date of her life. The insightful, intelligent, and noble man sitting across from her would have absolutely won her over, romantic that she was.

She had asked him about his occupation and discovered he and his friends were in the U.S. Navy, stationed on the east coast of the United States, in Virginia Beach. He'd been born in Connecticut, and he'd studied both American and Spanish Literature in college. As a junior officer, he outranked both Austin and Chuck, who were enlisted, yet he spoke of them as his equals. When she excused herself to use the restroom, he stood and pulled her chair back. And when she returned, he stood up again, flattering her with his respect.

As special as he made her feel, dread knotted her intestines, stealing her appetite. Sneaking peeks at her cell phone, she measured the time left before everything she'd ever known disintegrated.

As if it weren't distressing enough to think of her city ravaged, the innocent people about to be killed, Katrina's family would never be the same. Martí would never get away with what he and his comrades had plotted. Jordi, who'd known of the plan for a while and done nothing, would be dragged down with his brother. Katrina's conscience demanded she do something—fast, before it was too late. Yet fear and denial kept her in a state of paralysis.

What if talk of a bomb was merely that—talk? After all, Martí's friends had accomplished so little with their lives, was it even possible for them to coordinate properly and see their plans through without getting caught?

Aware that she ought to be conversing more, Katrina let Mitch fill the deepening silence. He did so by relaying the story of what happened to a teammate while on a cruise to Mexico. Under ordinary circumstances, the harrowing story would have enthralled her. That evening she could scarcely pay attention.

"Katrina?"

Jerking her gaze to his, she realized he had noticed her wandering thoughts.

"If you don't want to be with me, it's okay. I can take you home. No hard feelings."

His gentle assurance prompted a rush of guilt.

"No." She reached for his hand, scooting to the edge of her chair and causing their knees to bump. "It's not you," she assured him. In fact, the small part of her that was not preoccupied by her brothers' plot couldn't help but appreciate the warm density of Mitch's leg and the strength in the hand beneath hers. A sprinkling of hair rasped her palm as she slid her fingers up to his wrist and higher.

At the physical connection, the fear that had

constrained her up until then yielded to reason. She couldn't turn a blind eye to what she knew was coming. Meeting Mitch's puzzled gaze, she asked in a voice raw with fear, "What would you do if you knew something bad was going to happen and innocent people were about to get hurt, maybe even die?"

In his pupils, she could see the reflection of her pale face as he searched her expression.

"That's not a hypothetical question, is it?" His deep voice held an edge to it.

"What would you do?" she pressed, needing his support to do what was necessary.

"I would try to stop it."

There it was. Fear and relief plunged simultaneously into her midsection, followed by a desperate sense of urgency.

"What if that meant betraying people close to you?"

Empathy softened his features. He covered her hand with his free one.

"You have to do what's right," he told her steadily. "What's this about?" His tone left no room for her to lie to him, not that she felt the need to. With Mitch's help, she could make a difference.

With her heart galloping, she leaned across the table and whispered in his ear. "In fifteen minutes, a bomb is going to go off at the market, *La Boquería*, as a protest to Spanish oppression."

As he eyed her in astonishment, Katrina fall back into her seat, afraid he would look at her with condemnation. Instead, he pulled out his cell phone—clearly an automatic response—then realized it was useless to him.

"Here, use mine," she offered, finding it already in her other hand.

"Thanks." While tapping out a number, he managed at the same time to hail their waiter. "Haiku, where are you?" he demanded, taking the bill before Katrina could snag it.

His self-possession, his measured actions kept her panic from spiking.

"Are you near *La Boquería*, the big market we walked through twice already?"

She listened to him give directions to his colleague, lapsing into military jargon that made her suspect he'd had a great deal of experience in the field—not only on a boat. Interpreting his directions to Haiku, she deduced that his friend would find the nearest civil guard and convey the potential for an imminent explosion.

"I'll find you." Severing the call, Mitch handed Katrina back her phone. "Let's go," he said, leaving enough money to cover the tab. "What's the fastest way to the market?" he added, as he pulled her to her feet.

"This way." A glance at her phone had her breaking into a run. "It's seven minutes to six!"

The toe of her sandal caught on the lip of the curb. Mitch kept her from pitching face-first onto the sidewalk. In her urgency, she kicked off her sandals and left them right there on the street.

What if they were too late? What if the *Guardia Civil* didn't believe Haiku, or the market wasn't evacuated in time? *La Boqueria* was immense, the size of a soccer field. How long would it take to empty it of people? What if the bomb was still so powerful that even people on the street were devastated by its blast?

A minute later, they burst out of an alley onto *Las Ramblas*. To Katrina's amazement, the tree-shaded avenue appeared no different than it always did around six o'clock on a Sunday evening. Dozens of people, mostly tourists, populated the broad street enjoying the many restaurants and shops, kiosks and cafés. Not one of them had a clue what was about to unfold.

"There's Chuck." Mitch had spotted his colleague next to one of the immense poplar trees deep in conversation with a *benemérita*. Austin stood nearby. He waved Mitch over.

Mitch put both hands on Katrina's shoulders and spun her in the direction from which they'd come. "Go back to the hotel," he told her. Before she could say a word of protest, he was darting across the avenue, dodging pedestrians and kiosks to join his friends.

The realization that she'd put her three guests squarely in harm's way kept Katrina from complying with Mitch's request. She watched as he joined Chuck in addressing the civil guard. Talking earnestly, he showed the man his ID and passport.

A cold sweat breached the pores of her skin. There had to be *something* she could do. She could call Martí and beg him not to detonate the bomb.

With a sense of unreality, she dialed Martí's number only to listen to his voiced recording. Doubting he would hear her message in time, she left one anyway. "Martí, please don't do this. There are too many people. It's nothing but murder."

As she ended the call, she noted the time. Two minutes to six. How could the entire market be evacuated in just two minutes? Perhaps, by some miracle, Martí had already come to his senses and abandoned his plan.

A sudden stir took place at *La Boquería*'s wide entrance. The guard with whom Mitch had been talking barked into his radio. With broad gestures, he ordered several of his underlings to follow him into the dim interior, presumably to evacuate the place.

With her heart in her throat, Katrina saw Mitch,

Chuck, and Austin share a look amongst themselves. In one accord, they turned and followed the guards inside.

The blood drained from Katrina's head as she watched them disappear. "No!"

A sudden siren split the air, startling her into nearly wetting herself. Tourists and merchants alike began pouring out of the market. Looking anxious and confused, they called out frantically for their loved ones. A palpable wave of alarm rolled toward Katrina, even while her eyes remained fixed on the entrance for any sign of Mitch and his companions.

My God, how could she ever forgive herself if they got hurt?

Suddenly, with enough force to shake the cement beneath her feet, the very air seemed to splinter. The force of the blast knocked Katrina to her knees. Having expected it, she scrambled up again, wobbly on her feet, to stare at the smoke billowing out of the market doors.

"Mitch!" Without making any conscious decision to go after him, she found herself stepping over people. Through the muted buzzing in her ears, she could hear women and children wailing, car alarms blaring. Everywhere she looked there was debris and chaos but very little blood.

The blood would have been spilled *inside* the building where Mitch and his friends had gone in order to pull innocent people to safety.

Oh, God, please. Please, I will never ask for anything ever again. Just let them be okay.

CHAPTER SEVEN

"**G**o." Lifting himself off the old man he'd just covered when the bomb abruptly detonated, Mitch shook off the effects of the percussion and pulled the aged merchant upright. He then dragged the man through blinding smoke toward what he hoped was the exit. Passing him off to waiting hands, Mitch headed back into the blast zone, hunting for other survivors. Dread of a second explosion turned his mouth to dust.

Kicking plywood and plastic out of his path, he hunted for telltale traces of gore.

Thanks to the siren that had gone off seconds before and the wariness of the European population in general, the market had been mostly empty when the bomb detonated. Only a few stubborn merchants, like the old fish monger, hadn't wanted to leave their goods to potential looting and had stayed put.

Picking his way through the debris, while the lights flickered overhead from a compromised circuit—Mitch could hear Chuck, Austin, and the civil guards calling out like he was, creating a volley of Spanish and English.

"Is anybody here?"

"¿Hay alguien aquí?"

He flipped tables upright, peered over fallen display cases, and crunched through shattered glass. A hole in the corrugated metal ceiling showed where the bomb had been planted. Directly below it, the unsightly splatter of vegetables, fruits, olives, fish, and squid covered every conceivable surface.

Stepping through what smelled like pulverized cheese, he came abruptly across a body—or what was left of one.

"Over here," Mitch called to the nearest civil guard, who reared in alarm at the sight of him, grappling for his pistol and drawing it.

"*Tranquilo, tranquilo!*" Hands in the air, Mitch attempted to explain that he and his friends were helping.

The guard ignored him, summoning several others who grabbed hold of him and escorted him to the exit. Chuck and Austin had been likewise rounded up. The three of them were thrust into a corner to await questioning. Twenty minutes later, an officer in a red beret—beak-nosed and keen-eyed, ordered them with a crook of his finger to follow him back onto the street.

Once in the fresh air, Mitch directed his watering eyes to the place where he'd left Katrina. A perimeter was being erected to keep civilians at a safe distance. Several injured souls, some more seriously wounded than others, were being ushered to the line of ambulances pulling up on the next block over, their sirens blaring. The population had diminished substantially, suggesting people had fled the scene in dread of a second blast. He was glad not to catch sight of Katrina.

Suddenly, there she was, peeking at him from the other side of a saw-horse. As their gazes met, she sent him a tremulous smile, only to stiffen when a man caught her from behind and jerked her around. Mitch recognized her brother Jordi from the restaurant. Speaking to her briefly, Jordi thrust Katrina in the direction of the hotel. As she glanced back at Mitch, Jordi followed her gaze to intercept Mitch's watchful regard.

Recognition registered on Jordi's face. He had scarcely noticed Mitch at the restaurant the night before, but just now he seemed to recognize him.

An uncomfortable thought lodged in Mitch's mind. *What if Katrina's other brother suspected her interference? Would he retaliate?*

"Mitch." It was Austin, shaking him by the shoulder to get his attention.

The man in the red beret was waiting with an impatient scowl for them to keep up.

Starting forward again, Mitch heaved an inward groan. The *Guardia Civil* would want to know how he'd heard about the blast in the first place and why he'd waited so long to sound the warning. They would launch a full-scale investigation. The press might even get involved.

Commander Montgomery was going to shit bricks when the news out of Barcelona came to his attention.

PUSHING HER WAY into the hotel, Katrina found the marble-tiled foyer like the streets outside—strangely deserted on a Friday evening. Since the explosion, citizens and tourists alike had retreated into their homes and hotels for safety.

"Pare!" she called, spying her father's salt and pepper curls behind the check-in desk. She hurried toward him, intending to discuss the fate of her foolish brothers and how Martí's actions would impact them all.

To her bemusement, she found her father slumped in his chair, head and shoulders resting on the counter, fast asleep.

"*Pare!*" She gently shook him, astonished that anyone could be sleeping with the city in such a stir and sirens still blaring. Beneath her fingertips, his shoulder felt cool to the touch, his body strangely rigid. She snatched her fingers back, taking closer stock of his face. The bluish cast of his skin, his slack mouth and glazed, half-open eyes made her stagger backward in shock. "Pare!"

With the breath locked in her lungs, she stared at him. Coming on the heels of the explosion, it was too much to accept. Time stood still.

Ambulance! Call an ambulance.

Finding her cell phone in her hand, she thumbed 112 automatically, even knowing it would make no difference. In a thin, wavering voice, she told the operator to send an ambulance to Hotel Leonardo. Her father had suffered a stroke or a heart attack.

The operator hesitated. "I'm so sorry, *señorita.* Our emergency services are overextended at the moment. It will take some time for an ambulance to reach you. I can assist you in tending to the patient. Is your father breathing on his own?"

Katrina braced herself to look down at her father's still form. "No."

"Is his heart beating? Can you feel a pulse?"

With her stomach threatening to upend itself, Katrina reached over the counter to palpate her father's neck in search of a pulse. His skin felt waxen.

"No," she admitted, feeling nothing but cold tissue. "He's gone."

A long pause followed her whispered words. "To keep ambulances available to those who need them, may I send a medical examiner from the *Instituto de Peritaje Médico*?"

"Yes." Katrina's knees wobbled. The floor turned liquid beneath her feet, and she pivoted abruptly, sliding down the face of the counter to sit on the cold marble floor.

"You understand that the coroner is equally busy at the moment. Someone will come within the hour."

"I understand."

A steady tone had been coming from her phone for some time before Katrina put it away. A couple of hotel guests wandered in, their gazes sliding from her to the slumped body of her father. Not one of them hurried over to inquire what had happened. The evening's violence had apparently been too much for them, as well.

Mitchell would help her if he were here, came the errant thought. But he and his friends remained conspicuously absent. At least they weren't hurt in the blast, she comforted herself.

The hotel's front door opened again. Looking up, Katrina watched Jordi step inside. His progress faltered the instant he noticed her.

"What are you doing on the floor? Are you hurt?"

He started toward her only to catch sight of their father and stop again. "What's wrong with Pare?"

"He's dead." Katrina forced herself to say the words aloud. Tipping her head back, she glared at him accusingly. "I found him like this when I got here."

He swayed on his feet, visibly shocked. "No."

"The coroner is coming," Katrina added. With a portion of her own shock retreating, she found the wherewithal to climb to her feet. "Then again, it could be a while since the coroner is busy with the bodies of those killed in the blast today."

He cringed at her accusatory tone. His eyes darkened with both fear and resentment.

"That man at the market, the one who helped the *Guardia Civil*," he said, "I saw him last night at the restaurant. You told him, didn't you? You told him, and then he and his friends helped to clear the market before the bomb went off." His eyebrows came together, and he took a threatening step in her direction.

"No." She tried to deny it, but fear made her voice shake.

"Oh, Jesus." He wheeled away, clapping a hand to his eyes and muttering to himself. When he looked at her again, the skin on his face was blotchy. "When Martí finds out, he will kill you. And then he will kill *me* for telling you in the first place. Saint Jordi help us both," he cried, calling on the patron saint for whom he'd been named and revealing his reason for not alerting authorities in the first place.

Jordi was afraid Martí would kill him.

"Idiot," she raged as indignation flared in her suddenly. "What did you think would happen? Did you think he would get away with killing and maiming people, and you'd never have to tell anyone? No wonder Pare had a stroke. His sons are both idiots!"

Unable to wrap her mind around the madness of their situation, she gestured at their father. "*You* killed Pare. Don't you see that? Both of you, with your defiance and your obsession with independence. You killed him!" Her stricken voice echoed off the high ceiling.

"Enough!" he hissed, taking a threatening step in her direction. "Don't blame me," he pleaded. "I had nothing to do with it. It was all Marti's idea."

"Tell that to the *Benemérita* when they come calling," she hissed.

Tense silence stretched between them.

"You can wait for the coroner," she decided suddenly. The realization that she, too, would come under suspicion made her want to flee.

"Where are you going?" Jordi demanded as she

spun toward the door leading to their basement apartment.

"I don't know. I can't look at you." She darted through the door and down the steps to seek asylum in her bedroom.

CHAPTER EIGHT

FOR COUNTLESS MINUTES, Katrina lay face down across her narrow bed, overcome by grief, dismay, and uncertainty. Her father was dead. She knew from having lost her mother five years before that her life would never be the same.

The continual blare of sirens turned her shock into guilt. Recalling how Mitch and his companions had risked their lives to save others, she sat up slowly, wondering at their fate. Turning her head to look at the television she rarely ever watched, she rolled out of bed to turn it on, looking for news of the incident.

The voice of a local newscaster reached her ears. "…the three American servicemen who helped the civil guards clear *La Boquería* have been taken into custody for questioning."

With a gasp of surprise, Katrina increased the volume and stepped back to stare in consternation at a short clip of Mitch, Chuck, and Austin being forced into the back of a police van, their expressions grim.

"A radical separatist group called The Liberation Front has claimed responsibility for the bombing."

Katrina covered her mouth with a hand. Martí's group of misfits had made no secret of their involvement. Were they crazy? It was only a matter of time, now, before the *Benemérita* found and arrested Martí—maybe her and Jordi, also.

"As such, the three American servicemen are expected to be released. Locals here agree their quick thinking may have saved countless lives."

The screen flashed to a live view of the devastated market. "In the meantime"—the anchor's tone turned melancholy—"workers are continuing to sift through the explosion's aftermath in a hunt for survivors. The death toll continues to stand at four. Dozens of people are reported injured and at least two are confirmed missing."

Snapping off the television, Katrina turned away from it, unable to bear the thought that she should have acted sooner. Yes, Martí was ultimately responsible. Yet she, herself, could have gone to the authorities right away. Why hadn't she?

She had hoped Martí would come to his senses before it was too late.

A sudden pounding at her door made her jump.

Holding her breath, she waited.

"Katrina, open up!"

The sound of Martí's voice paralyzed her. The doorknob gave a jiggle. "I know you're in there. Jordi told me everything. He said you told the Americans of our plans."

She could hear him breathing heavily through the crack in the door.

"You know what happens now, don't you? Those Americans are going to tell the *Benemérita* how they knew about the bomb, and they are going to come here to question *you*."

Katrina shook her head. *No.* Mitch wouldn't betray her. How she knew him well enough to know that, she couldn't say. It didn't matter. Martí wouldn't believe her anyway.

"You'd better think of a story to tell those bastards, Katrina. If you betray me, I promise you, you *will* regret it."

The threat slid beneath her skin like the finest of razor blades.

With a final huff, Martí retreated.

Katrina sat heavily upon her bed, clutching a pillow to her roiling stomach.

"Pare," she whispered, breaking into silent sobs. "What do I do?"

Her father, her one constant, was no longer alive to comfort her as he had when her mother had passed, nor to advise her, the way he had when Armando had betrayed her trust. That betrayal paled in comparison to this current crisis. To what Martí had done to her family. What if Mitch *did* lead the *Guardia Civil* into questioning Katrina? In her guilt, she would tell them everything she knew and hope to be forgiven.

But then she would still have to deal with Martí, who would likely try to silence her before or after she betrayed him.

Katrina's thoughts went immediately to Mitch. Mitch could protect her.

Was it fair of her to ask him, though? Of course not. She had thrust him into the middle of a struggle that had nothing to do with him. She would protect herself. She would flee to the ski resort her family had frequented up until the winter her mother died.

Somehow, some way, she would hide from her older brother and start over.

MITCH SET A brisk pace as he and his teammates hurried from the Clinical and Provincial Hospital of Barcelona under the cover of darkness. Treated for abrasions and mild burns, they had slipped out of an employee-only exit to avoid the journalists waiting in the lobby.

Because of the bombing, the citywide curfew had

been rolled back to midnight.

"Step it up, guys," he urged, sneaking a peek at his watch. They had half an hour left to get back to their hotel before they found themselves in violation of the law—not a good idea considering they'd already fallen under the watchful eye of the federal police.

"How many blocks?" Austin asked.

"About six."

"Seven," Chuck corrected.

The scurrying of footsteps drew Mitch's head around. One block behind them, two men darted into the shadows, making it clear they didn't wish to be seen.

"We've got two on our tail," he warned. *Now what?* he thought.

Austin cocked an ear but didn't look back. Squaring his shoulders, he slid a hand into his front pocket, which no doubt held the knuckle ring he kept handy. Mitch felt for his own folding dagger and gave a thought to his backup blade.

"Stay cool," he ordered Austin. "We don't need any more attention at this juncture."

"Who do you think it is?" Austin asked.

Several possibilities came to mind. "Well, I think del Rey is keeping an eye on us," Mitch replied. The civil guard with the red beret had introduced himself as Capitán Rodrigo del Rey and taken them promptly into custody. Within the municipal police station, commandeered by the the federal police, del Rey had grilled them on how they'd come to hear about the bombing in advance of the explosion.

Conscious of the need to protect Katrina, Mitch nonetheless stuck as close to the truth as possible. "I overheard a conversation."

"Where?"

"At a bistro a couple blocks away, *La Granja.*" Versed in interrogation, he knew to supply specific details, just not those del Rey was looking for.

"All three of you were there?" the captain grilled.

"No, just me with some girl I met last night at Razzmatazz."

"The girl's name?"

"Katrina."

Del Rey looked up from the iPad he was typing on. "Katrina what?"

Mitch had shrugged and shook his head.

"So you were sitting there at *La Granja* and you overheard a conversation about a bomb." Del Rey's tone had sounded understandably skeptical. "Was the conversation in Spanish?"

"No," Mitch replied.

"Then you speak Catalán?"

The man had thought he was being crafty but Mitch was ready for the question. "The words *bomb* and *market* have Latin roots. I would have to be dense not to understand what was being said."

Del Rey had stared at him so hard a light sweat had dampened Mitch's button-up shirt. "Describe the men who were talking."

Mitch offered up a generic description, at which point del Rey had put his iPad aside and demanded to be put in touch with their commander. Fortunately, his subsequent conversation with Captain Montgomery had eased his suspicions sufficiently, as Montgomery had made it clear his SEALs had zero connection to The Liberation Front. In lieu of locking them up, del Rey had driven them to the hospital to have their minor wounds looked at.

"Stay in Barcelona," he had ordered as he'd dropped them off. "If I look for you at Hotel Leonardo, I expect to find you there."

They had wandered into the hospital only to run into a swarm of journalists. If not for the overprotective hospital staff, they'd have found themselves being interviewed, close-up shots of their faces televised worldwide. It was possible a couple of persistent journalists were trailing them even then.

There remained a third possibility—one that made Mitch's nape prickle. The look Katrina's brother had given him right after the bombing suggested that The Liberation Front, who'd claimed responsibility, might have a bone to pick with the three Americans.

"We need to get out of his city," Mitch murmured.

Chuck looked over at him. "Del Rey said we had to stay."

"In the hotel run by the separatists who blew up the market?" Mitch retorted. "No thanks."

"So, we vanish," Austin suggested. "We've all got our passports, right. We can go right now."

All they would leave behind was a couple changes of clothing. "Possible," Mitch agreed, though the thought of leaving without telling Katrina goodbye panged him. "There's just one problem. You see any taxis?"

Only a stray car or two still coursed the streets, and neither was a taxi.

"We could walk out," Austin suggested.

"We'd have to cover twenty klicks without being picked up by a civil guard."

"Then we're trapped like rats until the sun rises," Chuck determined.

Mitch felt strangely relieved. As they turned a corner toward the looming white walls of Hotel Leonardo, a handful of men came into view, closing around them as a semicircle that kept them pinned against the building.

"Oh, hell," he muttered.

"Ambush," Austin determined, as the two men on their tail cut off their exit. Dressed in street clothes, the hostile stances and unkempt appearance of their opponents identified them as members of the separatist group.

"Well," Chuck said, producing a *shuriken*, a throwing star, from his thigh pocket, "adversity introduces a man to himself."

Austin grinned at the prospect of a fight. "I like getting to know myself."

Mitch pictured Captain Montgomery's blistering response to an altercation. "No bodies," he ordered sternly, although the measures they would have to take depended entirely on the opposition.

Taking stock of them, Mitch figured the odds weren't as bad as they could be, all things considered. All the same, he would welcome interference on the part of the *Guardia Civil*—conspicuously absent when they were most needed.

"We heard about you on the news." The ringleader, a bald man in a leather jacket swaggered forward to address them in heavily accented English. Pulling back his jacket, he let them see the butt of an antique pistol holstered to his left side. "We are The Liberation Front," he announced. "You have no business interfering in matters that don't concern you."

Mitch wondered briefly if the man was Katrina's older brother, then decided he didn't resemble Jordi enough to be related. "Relax," he said. "We're leaving in the morning."

The separatist sent them a cocky smile. "No need to wait." He gestured to a dark windowless van idling just across the street. "We will give you a ride to the edge of town."

"Thanks, but we'll leave on our own," Mitch insisted. He couldn't be sure the separatists wouldn't drive the SEALs to some quiet location, then try to execute them. Besides, he was loathe to leave Katrina without first making sure she would be okay.

Predictably, the bald man drew his pistol. Mitch eyed the Astra 600 with interest. Manufactured in Spain as early as the 1920s, the 600 had been exported to Germany during WWII. The gun was a classic, but still just as accurate as in its heyday.

Mitch countered by flicking open his switchblade. The men behind them rushed at them suddenly. Ducking, Mitch hurled an assailant over his shoulder. Chuck leveled two opponents in the same instant, imbedding his *shuriken* at their thighs, and Austin kicked the Astra 600 out of the ringleader's hand. As it skittered across the street, the ringleader keeled over, a victim of Austin's famous right hook.

Mitch ran for the pistol, snatched it up, and aimed it at the three remaining separatists, who backed away with their hands up.

Mitch gestured for his friends to keep moving. "No hard feelings," he said to whomever could understand him. "Like I said, we'll be out of here tomorrow morning." Tucking the 600 into the waistband of his slacks, he joined his friends in walking away. Over their shoulders, they watched the uninjured separatists help their injured counterparts to the van.

Hurrying into Hotel Leonardo, all three SEALs cut a wary glance at the reception desk. The man seated behind the counter looked as old as Katrina's father—too old to be her brother—but he wasn't Felipe.

"Hold the elevator," Mitch requested, crossing to the reception desk. The sparse-haired stranger looked up from his cell phone.

His eyes rounded with recognition. "You're one of the Americans," he exclaimed.

Fantastic. They'd become overnight celebrities.

"Are you related to Katrina?" Mitch glanced at the man's nametag.

"No, no." Juan Carlos shook his head. "I moved here from Toledo. I only work for the Ferrer family when they're shorthanded."

"Why are they shorthanded?" Mitch was hoping to hear Katrina's brothers had been arrested.

"Ah." Juan Carlos shook his head sadly. "The owner of the hotel died of a heart-attack today. It happened around the time the bomb went off."

Mitch widened his stance at the unexpected

news. "Sorry to hear that. How's the family doing?"

Juan Carlos sighed. "They're upset, of course. I haven't seen any one of them all evening."

Mitch glanced around. "Do you have some way to reach Katrina?" he asked.

"Katrina?" The man shrugged. "Sure. I can text her."

"Yes. Can you do that now?" Mitch looked pointedly at the man's cell phone. "Tell her the Americans are leaving at dawn, and they asked about her," he added.

The thought of never seeing her again turned his feet to lead.

Juan Carlos thumbed the message painstakingly before hitting send.

Mitch held his breath, hoping to hear a quick reply.

The man looked up. "Would you like me to print your statement now?"

"Uh, yeah. That'd be great."

As the printer spit out the bill, Mitch strained his ears for the sound of a reply text. He signaled for his friends to hold the elevator a little longer.

"There you go." Juan Carlos handed him the printout. "I'm sorry if you have cut your vacation short," he added kindly.

"Me, too," Mitch said, then retreated from the desk to join his teammates. Sorrow and concern knotted his intestines. Was Katrina okay? Was it even safe for her to remain in Barcelona?

"The hotel owner had a heart attack today," he relayed as the elevator started upward. "He's dead," he added.

His friends blinked at him in atonishment.

"Man." Austin shook his head sympathetically. "How's Katrina doing?"

"No idea." Mitch could only imagine she was devastated—perhaps too consumed by grief to look after herself. If only there was something he could do to protect her, but he and his buddies weren't exactly in any position to help. Come dawn, they were going to slip away. After they left, he doubted he'd ever see or hear from Katrina again.

This day couldn't get any worse, he thought. Then the memory of the scuffle they'd just come from came to mind. Actually it could, he realized, if The Liberation Front risked the curfew to come after them tonight, bringing reinforcements.

CHAPTER NINE

KATRINA STRAINED HER ears for the sound that had awakened her. *Metal scraping over metal.* Her head came off the pillow as she lurched upright. In the darkness of her bedroom, her door was framed by a wavering light, as if someone out in the hall was holding a flashlight.

Martí. The realization of who was out there and why had her bolting out of bed. She'd been afraid he might attempt to force his way in. As a precaution, she'd stolen the master key from the reception desk, and now it seemed he was sawing his way in, perhaps with a hacksaw.

Panic streaked to her extremities. Considering her a traitor, her brother meant to get to her to do God knew what.

Quietly, she reached for the backpack she had stuffed with personal items ready for her early morning departure. As a precaution, she had gone to bed fully dressed. Grateful for her foresight, she jammed her feet into her favorite shoes, then stepped onto her bed, reaching for the narrow window over it. For years, it had served as her fire escape. Tonight, it would help her to escape the nightmare her life had become.

The hinge squeaked in protest, and the sawing at her door ceased.

"Katrina, open the door," Martí demanded.

The mad edge to his voice galvanized her. Tossing her backpack out onto the street, she wriggled through the casement after it. Cool air wafted from the sea. Shivering with fear, she shouldered her pack and moved quickly up the alley. *What now?*

Cruising the streets during curfew would ensure her arrest. The only safe place to go was right back into the hotel, using the master key she'd lifted. She would hide out until dawn.

Wishing there was another choice, she found herself minutes later standing at the door of Mitch's hotel room, out of breath from running up the stairs. Doubts assailed her. She had ruined his vacation. He had every right to deny her shelter.

A flicker of light drew her gaze to the buttons over the elevator. Someone was moving through the hotel—perhaps Martí. Fear convinced her to knock firmly on Mitch's door. Her heart thudded as she waited. A glance at the elevator showed that it was climbing.

What if Mitch and his friends had left already? Who could blame them? With no more time to deliberate, Katrina pushed the master key into the lock and shoved the door open.

Powerful hands hauled her into a pitch-black room, flung her around, and shoved her face-first into the wall. Something metal gouged her shoulder blade. The door clicked shut, and the light came on. Her assailant took one look at her and sprang away.

"Jesus!" The pistol he was holding disappeared behind his back.

Katrina calmed her racing heart as she took in Mitch's appearance. He was dressed entirely in black.

His blue eyes blazed with concern. "What the hell are you doing? I could have killed you!"

His two companions edged into the light, both dressed as he was—like special operators working a nighttime op. Recalling the way they'd handled that day's crisis, it came to her with sudden clarity that they weren't your average, everyday sailors.

"I'm sorry. I didn't know where else to go. Martí is after me," she admitted in a rush.

Urgency tightened Mitch's expression. "Does he know you're here?"

"I don't know. Maybe."

He snapped off the lights. "We need to move

out now," he said to his friends. "Grab your stuff."

"Where are you going?" Katrina asked, assuming they meant to leave her on her own.

"Anywhere but here," Mitch said, moving away to collect his possessions.

"But the curfew," she protested. "You don't want to tangle with the *Benemérita*, trust me."

"I'm open to suggestions. You got any ideas?"

Returning to her side, he curled a hand around her arm.

"Am I coming with you?" Relief made her question breathless.

"I'm sure as hell not leaving you here," he replied.

"Thank you!" She hugged him then—hard—and an idea came to mind. "I know a room here in the hotel where no one ever goes. And I have the only key," she added, realizing she still clutched it. "We can stay there until dawn. No one will bother us."

Mitch briefly considered the offer. "Better there than here," he decided.

A minute later, they darted into a deserted hallway. It must have been someone other than Martí moving through the hotel—perhaps Juan Carlos delivering room service. Leading the way to the sixth story, Katrina unlocked the penthouse suite. The curtains had been drawn half a decade earlier and never reopened. The smell of musty carpeting and stale linens made it evident no one used the room.

Using the lights on their cell phones, his team-mates swept inside taking stock of the place.

"Woah, this is nice," Austin called in a soft voice.

Mitch dumped his bag on the couch. "How come no one comes here?"

Katrina's throat tightened. "My parents lived here when they first got married. After I was born, we all moved to the basement where there's more space. After my mother died, Pare moved her belongings back up here and closed the suite to visitors." She didn't add that every year, on the eve of their anniversary, her father cloistered himself inside for days, mourning her mother's loss.

The reminder of Pare's recent passing impaled her suddenly. Sinking onto the sofa, Katrina buried her face in her hands and tried to come to terms with what was happening. She could hear Austin and Chuck murmuring to themselves as they located the second bedroom.

The cushion next to her yielded as Mitch sat be-side her and smoothed a large hand up and down her back.

"I heard about your father," he said softly. "I'm sorry."

The warmth of his palm, combined with his sympathy, compelled her to turn to him for comfort and security. His solid presence, the powerful arms encircling her, were a balm to her frazzled nerves.

"I'm so sorry," she whispered, her nose just inches from his neck. "I should never have involved you."

"You did the right thing." With that simple assertion he absolved her of her guilt. His arms tightened around her suddenly. "Will you let me help you?" he asked.

Her heart wrenched. Tears rushed into her eyes. "I don't know what to do," she admitted.

Mitch's heart thumped beneath her ear. "You can't stay in this city, Katrina. Members of The Liberation Front confronted us tonight. They're pretty pissed that we wrecked their little protest."

She lifted her head with alarm. In the dark, all she could make out was the clean lines of his all-American profile. "The *Benemérita* questioned you as well," she recalled.

"Just a formality," he assured her. "All the same, we've drawn a bit too much attention here. Time to move on and leave the populace to sort things out for themselves. You should come with us. We're going to Seville."

"Seville?" The historic town lay on the other side of the country, six hours away by high-speed train. Hope relieved the heavy weight on her chest.

"Yeah. And then we'll figure out what's next …

after that."

The words "after that" brought her fear right back. Of course, he hadn't been suggesting that she stay with them indefinitely.

"I was planning to go to Panticosta," she admitted. "It's a resort village where we used to take vacations. I have a lot of friends there, though I haven't been back since my mother's accident."

Mitch stiffened beneath her.

"That's the first place your brothers will look for you," he pointed out.

"Oh." Why hadn't she considered that? "You're right. I should go with you to Seville then…until I think of a better place."

"Yes. Good." He sounded relieved. Pressing a button on his watch, he added as it lit up briefly, "Four hours left until daylight. We should try to sleep."

Oddly, the thought of him making love to her held way more appeal than sleeping, but she knew he was right. Releasing him reluctantly, she pushed to her feet. Austin and Chuck had helped themselves to the second bedroom. "This way," she said, picking up her backpack and heading into the dark, adjoining chamber. Her mother's favorite quilt covered the queen-sized four-poster bed.

Mitch kept the door open and stowed his own bag on the dresser. "Keep the lights out," he reminded her as she reached for a lamp.

The comment drove home the danger they still faced. She stretched out on the bed, turning onto her side to stroke the material of the quilt beneath her. Memories of her mother drifted through her mind, drawing her gaze to the small picture frame on the stand next to her. She decided to take it with her, perhaps even tear off a portion of the quilt to keep as a memento. Grief tore through her at the thought that she might never return to Barcelona.

The bed dipped at her back as Mitchell reclined next to her. To her relief, he scooted closer, looping an arm around her waist and fitting himself snugly against the lines of her body.

"You're safe," he murmured. He had told her much the same thing when they'd left the nightclub together. Dear Lord, was that just twenty-four hours ago? He'd kept his promise then. She was certain he would keep it now.

How fortunate Mitchell Thoreau had come into her life when he had! Without his encouragement, who knew if she'd have had the courage to defy her brother in the first place. Part of her reasoned she should go to the *Benemérita* and turn him in. What better way to ensure Martí went to jail where he couldn't get to her? Who was to say, though, that the Civil Guard wouldn't charge her and Jordi with collusion? After all, they'd known about the threat and failed to act until it was virtually too late. The prospect of facing charges, of having her name linked to the bombing in any way, filled her with aversion.

Better to slip away with Mitch's help and avoid being associated, in any way, shape, or form to the radical movement.

MITCH RESIGNED HIMSELF to lying awake in bed. Unlike most SEALs, he could not sleep anywhere, any time. Stressful situations kept his adrenaline cycling, which kept him alert. The feel of Katrina curled so trustingly against him offered him a welcome distraction.

He let himself ponder her future and whether it had been irrevocably derailed by her oldest brother. The captain of the Civil Guard was no idiot. Del Rey had made a point of examining their cell phones to see whom they might have taken calls from just prior to the explosion. "Merely a routine precaution," he'd assured them.

One call in particular worried Mitch. He had called Chuck about ten minutes in advance of the explosion, using Katrina's cell phone. That call would have brought Katrina into del Rey's pool of suspects. Once the policeman learned her last name, he might well connect her to the radical separatist whose name was bound to come up as del Rey deepened his investigation. When that happened, he would most certainly want to question her.

The obvious solution was for Katrina to go straight to the authorities and tell them what she knew. She could offer to testify in exchange for physical protection. But then Mitch would never see her again. What's more, he'd traveled enough to know that political prisoners often disappeared, never to be seen or heard from again.

Social responsibility didn't always yield the best possible outcome, he reasoned. He could do more for Katrina by taking her away from the dangerous elements that threatened her. Not that his intentions were entirely selfless. He had to admit he wanted her to stay with him. He hadn't been ready to see the last of her—maybe he never would be.

If only he could shake the sneaking suspicion his decision to bring her along was going to cost him.

CHAPTER TEN

KATRINA STARED THROUGH the train window at the platform in dread of seeing Martí rushing up to the high-speed AVE, with the intent of dragging her off it. He would have to go through Mitch and his two friends first. Having witnessed their response to danger, her brother wouldn't stand a chance, she reassured herself. As the doors closed for the last time and the train began to creep from the station, she drew her first full breath and sat back.

Mitch, seated across from her, had been watching the platform, too. At one point, he had pressed his face to the glass, his gaze sharply alert. Whatever he'd thought he'd seen had apparently turned out to be nothing, for he'd eventually sat back, settled into his seat, and closed his eyes.

Across the aisle from them, Austin and Chuck had laid out a game of cards on the tabletop between them. As the train pulled away from the station, Katrina watched them for a moment, amused by their competitive natures. Losing interest, she entertained herself by studying a sleeping Mitch. His head lolled. His broad shoulders swayed gently with the rocking motion of the train. He looked younger in his sleep—perhaps no older than she was.

Guilt pressured her as she realized she was the reason for his weariness. He must not have slept as she had in the few hours preceding their flight from the hotel. Thinking back on their tense departure, she marveled that she had handled it as calmly as she had. Now that she could reflect on the fact that she'd left her home, perhaps forever, sorrow ambushed her. Turning her face to the window, she let tears fill her eyes and spill over.

Mitch slept on. Wiping her tears away, Katrina reconsidered him. The sun had risen behind the telephone poles running parallel to the tracks. Their shadows blipped across his countenance like frames in an old movie. Something about him inspired a deep respect and gratitude in her. The man had gone well out of his way, more than once, to help her.

Without warning, his head lifted and his eyes opened, jolting her with the sudden burst of color and with self-consciousness for having been caught staring. She jerked her attention outside again.

Having left Barcelona's suburbs, the train was streaking along the plateaus of the Central Depression at 125 kilometers per hour, making the backdrop look like a movie playing in fast-forward.

"You okay?"

The softly spoken question invited her into conversation.

"Sure." She sent him a brave smile, one that faded instantly as thoughts of her father's death and her present predicament entered her head.

"Ever thought about living in the States?" he asked.

Her pulse picked up. Was he inviting her? "Sometimes I have, yes," she said. "I have family in Kansas. I've used to visit them every summer when my mother was alive."

"Do you have dual citizenship?" he asked.

"Yes."

"What about a passport?"

"I have it with me. I renewed it last year for my vacation to Italy."

He guarded his thoughts behind an inscrutable expression. "Maybe you should visit your family in Kansas," he suggested.

Disappointment pricked her. "But there aren't many hotels where my cousins live," she protested. "That's what I do best—manage hotels." It had occurred to her there had to be dozens of hotels in a place like Virginia Beach.

"I'm pretty sure you could do anything you set your mind to," he said.

The affirmation warmed her, thought it wasn't quite the invitation she found herself hoping for. Distracted by a man stepping from the vestibule between the cars into theirs, she glanced up and her heart stopped. Dark eyes intercepted her astonished gaze. Armando froze in the act of reaching for the lavatory door. His gaze cut to Mitch, who looked over his shoulder and stiffened.

Snatching his hand back, Armando turned and exited their car at a near run.

Katrina met Mitch's grim gaze, her stomach churning.

"What's he doing here?" His tension had returned, making him seem suddenly years older.

Inwardly cursing their misfortune, Katrina moistened her dry lips. "He works for a franchise with offices in Zaragoza," she recalled.

"He's getting off at the next station, then," Mitch inferred, having obviously paid attention to their route.

"Yes."

"Do you think he'll tell anyone he saw you just now…with me?"

She wanted so badly to reassure him—to reassure herself—but knowing Armando, he would take serious pleasure in bad-mouthing her to her older brothers. "I'm afraid so."

To convey her sincere regret, she reached for Mitch's hand where it rested on the table between them and covered it. "I can get off too, if you prefer, and go back," she offered. "I'll turn myself in to the *Benemérita*."

One moment, her hand was on top of his; the next, it was firmly and gently trapped beneath it. "No," he said, calmly. "You're better off coming with us."

He sounded so certain, she didn't bother to argue with him. Besides, she had no desire to part company with Mitch. From the moment she'd first kissed him, she had felt like she belonged with him.

"Thank you," she whispered.

His small smile assured her he had heard her. Still, she noticed he couldn't bring himself to say, *You're welcome.*

FOUR HOURS LATER, they neared their destination with only one more stop—in Cadiz—before arriving in Seville. Mitch surveyed the dry, arid landscape of Andalusia, absorbing details as he'd been trained to, but his thoughts remained on the reflection he had glimpsed in a pane of glass covering a large, mounted advertisement at the station in Barcelona.

Could Capitán Rodrigo del Rey be following them?

One moment a dark pair of eyes had been staring at him out of the glass. Then people walked by, obscuring Mitch's view. When he could see the ad again, del Rey's reflection had disappeared.

Mitch tried telling himself he'd imagined it.

Something told him, though, that the man had traced the incoming number on Chuck's sat phone to Katrina Ferrer's cell phone. Subsequent research could have brought some very significant information to del Rey's attention, making him curious to know more.

Not for the first time, Mitch asked himself if bringing her along was a big mistake. It was one thing to remove her from the threat Martí presented. It was something else to associate himself with a person linked, albeit indirectly, to a terrorist act.

Yet on a personal level, he enjoyed her company immensely. Quiet and easygoing, she had napped for a portion of the journey, awakening in time to share the lunch he'd bought them from the food car. After thanking him, she had dug into her overstuffed backpack, produced a book, and lost herself in its pages.

As she read, she nibbled on her lower lip. The memory of the kisses they'd shared awakened the hope that he'd soon be kissing her again.

But what if del Rey *was* following them? Mitch's disquiet refused to leave him. Running into Armando at the outset of their trip had struck him as a seriously bad sign.

When they arrived in Seville, a day earlier than scheduled, he'd be smart to offer up a different credit card than the one he'd used to make all three of their reservations. That way, del Rey would have a harder time tracking them down.

As Katrina adjusted her stance, Mitch caught a glimpse of the cover of the book she was reading. "Wait." Astonishment rooted him.

She glanced up inquiringly.

"Are you reading *Walden*?"

She blinked in confusion then showed him the cover.

A smile of incredulity overtook him. "Did you notice the author's name?"

She flipped to the cover to read it. "Henry David Thoreau."

"Yeah, that's my last name. He was my great, great uncle."

Her eyebrows shot up. "Are you teasing me?"

He skeptical expression drew a robust laugh out of him. At the same time, he welcomed the sign that everything would be okay.

"Not this time," he assured her. "But I reserve the right to tease you in the very near future."

His response brought a blush to her cheeks.

"Don't move," he said, finding his cell phone.

She eyed him mistrustfully "What are you do-ing?"

"I'm taking your picture." That was about all his phone was good for overseas.

"Oh, no," she protested. "I look awful. I haven't washed my hair."

"Quiet. You're beautiful," he insisted. The bright Andalusian sun had turned the highlights in her hair to gold. "Smile for me," he requested, pulling a self-conscious smile out of her as he captured his shot.

Mitch put his phone away, glad to have a me-mento of her in the event he was left with nothing more. Whether they ended up together wasn't a question he could answer at the moment. All he knew was he intended to make her his in whatever time was left to him.

CHAPTER ELEVEN

A FIERY ORANGE sunset shimmered on the canal fronting Seville's *Plaza de España*, burnishing the face of the extravagant semicircular landmark. The grand structure, with its Moorish and Renaissance revival elements, had been featured as a backdrop in a recent *Star Wars* movie, making it famous overnight. Eying the forty-eight flags that represented the provinces of Spain, Katrina wondered if Catalonia's flag would flutter on its pole much longer.

"Want to rent a boat?" Mitch asked her. He had propped his forearms on the stone balustrade to watch rowboats gliding lazily along the canal and under the arched bridges.

Considering how much he had already splurged on a horse-drawn carriage ride through the historic district, Katrina shook her head. "That's okay. It'll be dark soon."

MARLISS MELTON

Straightening, Mitch put his arm around, drawing her close, the way he'd held her on the carriage. Together, they watched couples and young families pulling on the oars, doing their best to maneuver about the watery enclosure.

Katrina basked in the security of his embrace, the warmth of the moment. Being with him—it felt perfect.

"I love the water," he said on a reflective note. "In fact, I built a little house on the water. Want to see it?"

Her heart gave a funny leap at the question but then she realized he meant a photo of the house, not the house itself, as he removed his arm to pull out his cell phone. Accessing his photos, he paused briefly over the one he'd taken of her. "Pretty." Casting her a smile of appreciation, he then thumbed through his album to find the one he was looking for.

"Here." He showed it to her.

The tiny timber structure, standing under towering oaks and surrounded by blooming azaleas, intrigued her. She looked up at him. "Were you inspired by your great, great uncle?"

"Actually, yes. I built it myself," he added on a humble note.

She looked back at the photo in astonishment. "By hand?"

"Every bit of it. Don't get too excited. It doesn't have electricity."

"Is it on Walden Pond?" She regarded it more closely, having glimpsed a body of water beyond the house.

"No." He laughed softly. "It's on a man-made lake in North Carolina, about an hour from where I live. But it's still a great getaway. I go there to decompress."

His words spoke volumes about the harrowing nature of his job. Katrina checked her peripheral vision to make certain no one could hear her. "You're not an ordinary sailor, are you?" she asked, then looked him in the eye.

He had glanced up from his cell phone, his body perfectly still. "No," he said slowly. "I'm a Navy SEAL."

Though she suspected as much, his words sent a strange shiver through her.

"Does that put you off?" he asked.

She inhaled a shaky breath then slowly released it. "No," she decided. "My mother's skiing accident taught me to live life in the moment." The recollection of her father's more recent death hit her anew, causing her heart to compress and tears to rush into her eyes.

Mitch reached for her, stroking the side of her face to convey his sympathy. Katrina's sense of belonging transformed in that moment into a knowing. *This* was the man she was meant to be with. Closing her eyes, she nuzzled her cheek against his palm, then kissed it.

"I must be dreaming you," Mitch said, his words a reflection of her thoughts.

The sound of flamenco music and the warm, dry breeze fluttering the many flags conspired to serenade them. Heeding an inner voice, Katrina stood on tiptoe, encircled Mitch's neck with both arms, and pressed her lips to his.

They had not kissed since the night they'd gone out dancing. Scarcely forty-eight hours had passed since then, yet it seemed like a lifetime ago. His lips, she relieved to find, were both familiar and inviting. His sensual skill hadn't been a figment of her drunken imagination, then.

As warmth flowed through her, she melted against his solid frame. With her breasts pressed against his chest, she could feel the swift, powerful strokes of his heartbeat. He kept himself firmly controlled, but his voice rasped with desire as he spoke against her lips.

"I think we'd better head back to the hotel."

The prospect of intimacy stripped the air from her lungs. Catching up her hand in his, he led her briskly away from the canal in the direction of El Abanico Hotel.

As they strolled along the medieval streets of Seville, traversing diagonal alleys hemmed in by whitewashed buildings, Katrina lost her bearings. Had they gone left or right when leaving the hotel earlier that afternoon? The *Catedral*, looming over the red tiled roofs behind them, had been their clear landmark then. However, with the cathedral behind them, finding their way back to El Abanico proved trickier.

"Are you sure we're headed the right way?" she asked Mitch as they came upon a deserted plaza. Three narrow streets fanned off in three different directions. The sun had dropped behind the building at their back, leaving them with mere minutes left of daylight.

"Nope." He cast her a sheepish smile but then consulted his watch, which she realized had a compass on it.

"I could ask for directions," she offered, glancing around for an open shop.

"That's okay." He squeezed her hand affectionately. "I like getting lost with you." With confidence, he drew her toward the street on their right.

Katrina's heart fluttered. *Cuidado,* she warned herself. Mitch was not the self-interested bastard Armando was, but she should not overlook reality. The fact was, they were both persons of interest skirting a national investigation.

At the same time, she admitted she was falling in love. Mitch clearly felt the same way. At check-in, he'd requested an upgrade to a suite, giving them their own private bedroom. This night would be theirs alone. Regardless of what happened to them, she was certain she would cherish the memories they would make for years to come.

SEEING EL ABANICO Hotel with its lights glowing invitingly on the next street corner, Mitch breathed a sigh of relief. Compass or no compass, the maze of old roads and alleys would have challenged even the most directionally astute. Slanting Katrina a triumphant smile, he received a look from her that caused his testosterone to spike. The rest of the evening belonged to them. He would spend the whole night making love to her.

Picturing the queen-sized bed awaiting them, in a room decorated to reflect the era in which Miguel Cervantes wrote *Don Quixote*, Mitch swept open the hotel's massive door and gestured for Katrina to proceed him. As they crossed the foyer, designed to resemble an outdoor courtyard, his gaze collided with that of a man seated at one of the small coffee tables, and his expectations for a night of intimacy detonated without warning.

"Shit," he growled, slowing his step as he considered—and dismissed—the idea of trying to run from the law.

Glancing at him askance, Katrina followed his gaze to the man who was now rising from the table. The captain of the Civil Guard had put aside his red beret and uniform in favor of civilian clothing. Katrina's indrawn breath suggested she had managed to guess his authority.

"Lieutenant Thoreau." With a keen glitter in his nearly black eyes, Capitán Rodrigo del Rey intercepted their trek to the elevator. He extended a hand to Mitch, who grudgingly shook it. He had to respect the man's ability to tail him while being spotted only once.

"Captain." Resignation kept his tone flat.

Del Rey's gaze flickered over Katrina. "You've been enjoying Seville's many delights, I trust."

Mitch noticed he did not ask for an introduction, which meant he already knew who Katrina was. "It's a beautiful town," Mitch replied.

"Yes, it is." With a tip of his head, Del Rey indicated the table where he'd left his coffee. "Let's talk," he invited. "All three of us," he added, affirming Mitch's guess.

Katrina's silence bespoke her fear. She sent Mitch a scant nod, and they crossed to del Rey's table. Mitch pulled out a chair for her, while del Rey crossed to a sideboard to pour two additional cups of coffee. He brought them to their table, and both men sat.

"Creamer? Sugar?" These were already on the table. Del Rey pushed them closer to Katrina, who stared at her cup, unmoving.

Del Rey then sat back, hands interlaced on the tabletop while Mitch methodically doctored his coffee. The captain waited for Mitch to take his first sip.

"I told you to remain in Barcelona." The reprimand held only the slightest hint of recrimination, as if the captain hadn't expected his wishes to be followed anyway.

Returning his cup to the table, Mitch considered his reply. "When we left the hospital, on our way back to our hotel, my friends and I were confronted by members of The Liberation Front."

From the corner of his eye, he noted Katrina's startled response.

"They wanted to...escort us out of town in a van," Mitch added, downplaying what had actually taken place.

"Yes. I watched that happen."

"Ah." With the clarity of hindsight, Mitch realized *that* was why the street had been devoid of civil guards. Del Rey must have ordered them to clear the area hoping some event would unfold that would give him insight into the SEALs' role in the bombing.

With a small smile, del Rey acknowledged Mitch's thoughts. His dark gaze then settled predictably on Katrina.

"Ms. Ferrer. That is your name, is it not?" he addressed her mildly.

Katrina's sun-kissed face had lost all trace of its tan. She darted a frightened look at Mitch before holding del Rey's gaze and nodding. "Yes."

The captain shifted deliberately into Spanish, an obvious ploy to exclude Mitch. His quickly uttered observations were marked with the Castilian lisp typical of Spaniards from Madrid. Still, Mitch managed to decipher half of what he said— something about Katrina's allegiance to Catalonia, to her brothers.

"I'm not a member of The Liberation Front," she insisted, answering in English for Mitch's benefit.

Mitch laid his arm deliberately along the back of her chair.

Flicking him a look, del Rey seemed to accept her assertion. In the very next breath, however, he inquired as to whether she knew about the explosion in advance.

Katrina had knotted her hands in her lap. "Yes," she said in a strangled voice. Her eyes grew bright. "I forced my brother Jordi to tell me. He had nothing to do with it, I promise you. I'm sure he even told me in the hopes that I would do something—which I did. I told Mitch." Her gaze darted to him. "And he and his friends went straight to the *Benemérita*."

Continuing in Spanish, del Rey managed to extort the details she was reluctant to expose—like *when* Jordi had told her about the bomb and *when* she had relayed the truth to Mitch. He asked if Katrina didn't feel responsible for the lives that were lost as a result of withholding information from the authorities.

As tears welled in her eyes and her tightly held expression started to crack, Mitch pushed his chair back and stood up. "All right. That's enough."

Del Rey responded with a glance toward the stairs that drew Mitch's attention to a second man, unnoticed until that moment. He was coming down the marble staircase that descended from the second-story gallery enclosed by a wrought iron railing. Del Rey had brought along reinforcements—of course he had.

"Look." Mitch laid a comforting hand on Katrina's shoulder and registered her quaking. "Miss Ferrer isn't guilty of anything," he insisted, certain he spoke the truth. "You have a family, don't you, *Capitán*?" he demanded, keeping one ear cocked to the approach of the second civil guard.

"I do," del Rey admitted. A hint of amusement rode the line of his thin upper lip.

"Then you understand loyalty to family," Mitch continued. "Put yourself in Katrina's shoes. What would you have done? Betraying your own brother takes courage, especially when he threatens you, which he did. She defied Martí by telling me the truth. She saved a lot of lives in the process. Don't you dare lay guilt at her feet."

Squeezing his hand with ice-cold fingers, Katrina conveyed her gratitude.

Del Rey waved off the second man, keeping Mitch from getting any more defensive. With a grimace of acknowledgment, del Rey reconsidered Katrina, who held his gaze pleadingly.

"I see your point, Lieutenant."

The words eased the tight band around Mitch's chest. Katrina drew a shaky breath.

"Tell you what," the captain added, signaling for Mitch to sit and stop towering over the table.

He sank back into his seat, heart thudding as he awaited del Rey's decision.

"I will make the two of you a promise if you will make me one, in return."

Mitch caught Katrina's hope-filled glance. "What's your promise?" he asked.

"I give you my word I will protect Katrina from retribution at the hands of The Liberation Front, and I will see that she is not charged with any crime." He pinned Mitch with a look reminiscent of Captain Montgomery's default expression. "*You* will promise not to disappear tonight, as I myself could use some rest. Tomorrow at eight in the morning, you will hand Katrina into my custody. She is a key witness to a crime that has rocked the entire country. I cannot let her walk away—not until justice has been served."

Katrina's soft whimper tore at Mitch's heart-strings. Clearly, he hadn't been the only one hoping against all logic that she would end up going to the States with him—that they would stay together in the days, weeks, and months to come.

"It's okay," he murmured, reaching for her hand.

"Your word, Lieutenant?" del Rey prompted.

Squeezing Katrina's fingers reassuringly, Mitch conveyed to her that it would be all right. Del Rey was going out of his way to keep things civilized. He released Katina and rose slightly out of his seat to extend a hand across the table, sealing their arrangement.

"My word, *Capitán,*" he agreed.

"Go to your room, then," del Rey ordered. The look he divided between them was not without understanding and sympathy. "The night is still yours."

CHAPTER TWELVE

N O SOONER HAD the door of their suite clicked shut than Katrina turned to Mitch and threw herself against him.

The ferocity of his embrace let her know his emotional state was similarly distraught. But whereas she was being made to return to Barcelona to testify, Mitch was free to continue his vacation as if nothing had happened. Maybe, if he hadn't been a SEAL, he'd have been detained and made to bear witness, but his job apparently gave him immunity.

Between the two of them, her plight was most certainly worse.

"Listen," he finally said, cupping her face so she was forced to meet his gaze. "This is going to be behind us one day. We need to hold onto that thought."

She nodded in agreement even as her throat closed with sorrow.

"I'm not going to forget you," he added, his voice roughening. "I'm going to keep abreast of everything that happens. We'll keep in touch as much as we're able. And when it's all over, we'll see each other again."

Too choked up to speak, she forced a smile of gratitude.

"I want to give you something," he decided, releasing her suddenly to cross to the desk in the suite's living room. Rifling through the drawer, he located a pen, paper, and an envelope. She neared him in time to see him scribble a physical address and, below that, an email address.

Slanting her an enigmatic look, he moved into their bedroom, and she trailed him, watching as he pulled a set of keys from his duffel bag. He worked a single key off the key ring, folded it into the sheet of paper, then slid the paper into the envelope, sealing the key inside by licking the adhesive. He handed her the envelope.

"What's it for?" she asked.

"It's a key to my cabin, along with the address and my email. Write to me when you can. I want you to meet me there when this is over."

Hope buoyed her spirits as she lifted her gaze to his. A portion of her despair left her. "You have another key at home?" she guessed.

"Several," he said reaching for her again and

stroking her arms from shoulder to elbow. "I want you to know you have a place to call home when this is over. You can stay in my cabin as long as you need to. It's a healing place."

The intimation that she would need to heal after her ordeal brought her dismay rushing back. At the same time, cautious hope lent her unexpected resolve. She and Mitch still had a shot at a future together. She needn't give up on them entirely. Laying the envelope aside, Katrina embraced him a second time while looking him in the eye.

"Thank you," she said, keeping her sorrow in check for now. Their time was too precious to waste on tears.

His blue eyes blazed with emotion. With a muttered word of lament, he kissed her, crushing her lips beneath his, pulling her body close as if to sear the memory of her onto his senses. His feverish hands brought a whimper of want up her throat. Lifting her suddenly off her feet, he carried her several steps to the bed, spilled her gently on the mattress, then lowered himself over her.

Katrina melted under his welcome weight. Wrapping her jean-clad thighs around him, she aligned her hips with his, gasping at the jolt of pleasure that went through her when their bodies came together. Every nerve strained for his possession. Her heart raced, fueling her need for air.

"Mitchell," she murmured, burning with desire for him.

Jackknifing to his knees, he released the button of her jeans, tugged at the zipper, and then, with one determined movement, stripped her jeans down her legs. His open mouth followed their descent, searing against her bare skin as he nibbled and kissed her from her knees to her thighs.

Katrina had to bite her lip to keep her cries in check. Sinking her fingers into his thick hair, she climbed the rungs of pleasure, willing each moment to last while yearning for fulfillment.

"Oh, God!" His fingers, lips and tongue found their way beneath her panties. He teased her into a state of mindless rapture.

"Wait!" It was happening too quickly. She longed to slow it down, to revel in the moment. "I want you with me," she insisted, tugging him upward.

He stood up, undressing swiftly. Katrina watched in fascination as his shirt came off, exposing a chest rippling with muscle and dusted with light-brown hair. As he bent to pull his jeans off his feet, she glimpsed lean hips and powerful thighs. He stood up, displaying an arousal that was both beautiful and proud.

Before joining her on the bed, he rummaged in his bag, withdrawing a packet of condoms.

"Oh," she said, having given no thought whatsoever to protection.

With a seriousness that brought back the memory of her situation, Mitch tore open a wrapper and sheathed himself. Then he glanced up, sending her a look that curled her toes and made her tingle all over. In the next moment, he was looming over her, blocking her view of the iron chandelier hanging from the ceiling. She closed her eyes as he settled over her and tenderly kissed her. With hungry hands, she explored him, running her palms over his delightfully smooth skin, intrigued by the terrain of muscle and sinew beneath.

He kissed her, returning her to the same feverish state she'd been in just prior.

"Look at me," he breathed against her lips. He was poised to enter her.

Her blood flashed hot as she met his. The smooth head of his sex nudged her opening simultaneously. Watching her response to him, he sank slowly, inexorably into her, filling her so completely, with such focus, that her eyelids fluttered closed once more.

Withdrawing and filling her again, he drew a cry of abandon from her lips. "Mitchell!"

"Yes, baby," he gritted, sounding like a man in pain.

Catching her straying hands, he drew them over her head and pinned them to the pillows. Then, responding to her desperation, he drove himself into her, launching her pleasure to the stratosphere.

Katrina strained to greet each deep stroke. The muscles in her body tightened. Having felt him like this, she would never let him go. She would treasure him in her heart, and in her soul, forever.

"I love you," she heard herself cry as her climax claimed her suddenly.

With a growl, he surged into her one more time, burying his face in her hair and succumbing to his own release. They shuddered simultaneously, deeply joined.

With his heart still pounding against her breasts, Mitchell lifted his head and met her gaze.

"I love you, too," he said, sounding a bit bemused.

This moment, Katrina thought. This was the moment she would revisit in the weeks, the months of loneliness ahead of her. She would replay it again and again, feeding on the memory, recalling Mitch's earnest expression to give her courage; the memory of how it felt with their limbs entwined, still relishing the aftershocks of pleasure.

I will feel this way again, she swore to herself. *This will not be the end.*

AT 7 A.M., Mitch traced the delicate line of Katrina's

spine to rouse her from her slumber. They had both slept fitfully, finding solace from impending doom in the delights of getting physically acquainted. He'd never experienced such perfect chemistry before.

Their night together—as haunted as it was by the specter of dawn—had sealed his decision to wait for her. She would come to him when the trial was over, when The Liberation Front ceased to pose a threat to anyone.

If only he could be certain del Rey would keep his promises. What if Katrina was charged, after all, with colluding with her brothers? She could be sentenced to years in prison. How long was Mitch willing to wait? Or what if members of The Liberation Front found some way to strike back at her, in spite of del Rey's protection? Could the captain really keep her safe, or was that feat beyond the limits of his powers?

Mitch's worries, plus the added distraction of Katrina's naked body, had kept him from sleeping. Then, too, Austin and Chuck had swept into their shared suite around two in the morning. Mitch had rolled out of bed to apprise them of Katina's situation, his news putting a damper on their high spirits.

Mitch glanced again at his watch—7:10. "It's time to get up, sweetheart," he murmured. Del Rey wasn't going to give them a minute past eight before he came after them.

Issuing a moan of protest, Katrina turned to face him. Hooking a thigh around his hips, she snuggled as close to him as was feasible, making him regret that they'd depleted his modest stash of condoms. As much as he longed to make love to her again, he wasn't about to compound her uncertain fate by leaving her pregnant.

Skin to skin, he rocked her gently as she issued a sob against his neck.

"It's going to be all right," he murmured. "You'll get through this. Eventually it'll all be behind you, and you can come find me. I'll be waiting," he added. "I'll wait as long as it takes." Hearing himself make that promise, he knew it was the right one.

Sniffing, she tipped her head back. Just enough pearly light fringed the shutters for him to make out her beautiful features.

"I've never met anyone like you," she murmured. With trembling fingers, she traced the lines of his face as if to memorize them.

The lump in his throat kept him from answering. He was about to reiterate the need to rise when she pressed her lips to his, pulled away, and rolled with resignation from the bed to meet her fate.

CHAPTER THIRTEEN

D EL REY WAS waiting for them. He sat at the same table he had occupied the previous night, this time in his uniform, red beret perched just so atop his coal-black hair. Seated across from him was the second man—also in uniform, with a patch on his shoulders that suggested he was a sergeant of some sort.

The pair looked up at Mitch and Katrina as they emerged from the elevator, then went back to their breakfasts, clearly pleased not to have to fetch them. Carrying Katrina's backpack over his left shoulder, Mitch led her to the breakfast bar.

"You should eat something," he encouraged as she eyed the pastry display apathetically.

"I'm not hungry."

Mitch reached for a plate with his free hand. That very instant, the familiar crack of a bullet shattered the peaceful quiet. Del Rey and his sergeant exploded from their seats. Katrina slammed into the counter next to Mitch and bounced off, dragging a tray of pastries down on top of her as she collapsed onto the terracotta tiles. Her head struck the floor before Mitch could prevent it. He threw himself over her, fully expecting another round to be discharged.

Crack! The second shot struck tile, mere inches from their skulls, splintering ceramic and leaving his ears ringing. Mitch groped for the Astra 600 he had slid into the waistband of his jeans at the last minute before they left the suite. Pulling it out, he assessed Katrina briefly, noting her slack features, her closed eyes. A circle of blood bloomed on her left shoulder. *Jesus.*

He turned his head, taking the lay of the land.

Del Rey and his subordinate were taking refuge against the far wall, which put them immediately under the shooter, with no direct line of fire. All the same, the sergeant had drawn his weapon and was darting out of his hiding place to keep the shooter distracted.

Crack! Crack! Pits of plaster and tile rained down into the courtyard.

"Move!" Del Rey gestured violently for Mitch to take cover.

The depth of their vulnerability wasn't lost on Mitch. But, depending on the type of bullet lodged in her shoulder, moving Katrina could send it straight to her heart. Lunging for the base of the nearest table, Mitch jerked it hard and toppled it, dragging it close enough that the tabletop shielded them.

Still crouched, he thumbed off the Astra's safety and aimed it at dark head peeking around the pillar on second-story gallery. He took a bead and fired, discharging a round and imbedding it in the old brick just inches away. Dismayed by his inaccuracy with the unfamiliar weapon, he adjusted his aim and fired again. *Sshh-clenk.* The pistol jerked. Mitch willed his aim back to point then realized the second round had lodged against the spent shell of the first. The gun had jammed, making it useless.

A cold sweat enveloped him as he reset the safety and set it down. He and Katrina were sitting ducks. Glancing down at her, he found her alarmingly pale, the stain on her shirt wider.

"Hey, asshole."

Mitch's hopes rocketed as Austin's taunt echoed off the walls of the courtyard. *Oh, thank God.* His teammates had roused to the sound of shooting and naturally headed right for the trouble.

"What the fuck, dude? You're waking everybody up."

Mitch peered over the tabletop up to see a shirtless Austin ambling along the gallery with his hands outspread, no weapon in sight. What looked like sheer stupidity was, in fact, a distraction. Just then, the elevator slid open on the other side of the shooter, revealing an equally shirtless Chuck.

The shooter hesitated, uncertain of whom to fire at first. With a sweep of his hand, Chuck hurled one of his *shuriken*. The metallic stark-shaped blade struck its target in the chest. With a scream of agony, he sank to his knees, dropping his weapon.

Both SEALs ran at him. Austin pegged him to the ground, and Chuck kicked the man's pistol under the railing. As it fell with a clatter onto the courtyard floor, del Rey's sergeant retrieved it, then charged up the stairs to assume control of the situation.

Mitch scarcely recognized his strangled voice as he shouted to del Rey, "Call an ambulance! Katrina's hit!" Pushing away the overturned table, he hovered over her, releasing the upper buttons of her blouse to assess the bullet wound. The point of entry was more than an inch across; the slug had gone deep into her chest.

"No, no," he muttered. Shock threatened to slip over him, cold and numbing. Falling back on his training, he kept it at bay by feeling her pulse at her throat, talking to her to keep her present, and praying.

On more than one op, he'd taken Bullfrog's

place as the acting medic. As such, he'd treated several bullet wounds, but never on a woman he cared for. And never one that looked so fatal.

Grubbing in her backpack for something to use as a compress, he found a soft white T-shirt and pressed it to the wound. Palpating her wrist, he counted her weak heartbeats, while listening to her shallow breaths.

Without warning, she gave groan. Her eyelids fluttered, and she blinked up at him.

The disoriented and pained look in her eyes tore at his heartstrings.

"Hey, baby," he crooned. "Don't move," he added as she lifted her head to assess her situation. Almost immediately, her eyes rolled back and she passed out again.

Mitch swallowed a howl of frustration. "Come on, Katrina. Stay with me," he pleaded.

Not so much as a flicker of acknowledgement.

"Damn it, don't leave me. Look at me!"

The memory of her looking at him when they'd made love last night blew through his mind. Her eyes remained closed. His heart felt too heavy to beat.

Del Rey joined him, dropping onto his knees next to him with a look of shocked dismay. "Is she—?"

"She's alive." Mitch bit out the words, doubling

the pressure on her wound. "Where's the ambulance?" he demanded.

"They're on their way—five minutes." Del Rey's phone was still pressed to his ear.

Sparing a glance for the action taking place on the gallery, Mitch noted the sergeant wrestling the shooter into a pair of handcuffs. The man wailed in agony while shouting what sounded like "*Desperta Ferro!*" along with intermittent invectives.

"I'm so sorry," del Rey said, as he put his phone away.

Mitch couldn't look at him. "Is that her brother, Martí?"

"I believe so," the captain affirmed. "We've had a warrant out for his arrest. If I'd realized he would follow her here..."

"It's not your fault."

But it could be mine, Mitch acknowledged miserably. Katrina had warned him Armando was likely to tell her brothers what he'd seen on the train. Mitch should have sensed Martí Ferrer long before that man ever opened fire. If she died on him...

He refused to accept that outcome. "She'll be fine," he insisted.

"Yes, of course. I hear the ambulance," del Rey said, standing up to greet the paramedics at the door.

Ten minutes later, Mitch tried to follow the gurney carrying Katrina into the back of the ambulance.

One of the paramedics jumped in his way. "Are you her husband?" he demanded.

Mitch hesitated then ground out, "No."

"I'm sorry," said the man, firmly but with sympathy. He turned away and proceeded to close himself inside the vehicle.

"Wait, take her backpack. It has her ID in it."

"I'll take that," del Rey said, wresting it from Mitch's grasp and turning away.

Mitch pursued him. "Give me a ride," he demanded. "I need to stay with her."

With an audible sigh, del Rey turned back to speak with him. They stood on a narrow sidewalk being gawked at by pedestrians. Austin and Chuck had finished dressing and joined him, standing on either side like faithful bookends.

Dividing a gentle look among the three of them, del Rey gestured toward a van with a camera mounted atop it creeping up the cobbled street. "Are you sure you want to stick around? When the press realize the same men who prevented a massacre in Barcelona just saved a young woman's life in Seville, you're going to get far more attention than you bargained for."

Mitch didn't give a shit about attention. "We'll deal with it. Just take me with you," he exhorted.

All at once Chuck's sat phone gave a shrill ring.

Tensing, Mitch looked over as Chuck took the call.

"Suzuki."

It was often hard to tell what the unflappable Haiku was thinking, but the way his dark eyes darted first to Mitch then to Austin, Mitch knew with a plummeting of his heart that Spec Ops was calling. Some unforeseen occurrence necessitated their immediate return—a hazard they had all learned to accept in their line of work.

"Roger that. On our way." Chuck hung up.

Del Rey was astute enough to pick up on their new orders. He laid a firm hand on Mitch's shoulder. "Go," he said. "I'll take good care of her."

The doors of the ambulance shut with a clang, wresting Mitch's attention toward the red cross emblazoned on the back. Austin and Chuck shifted wordlessly closer as the vehicle pulled away, turning at the next corner. A second ambulance carrying Martí Ferrer chased silently after it, its red lights sparkling, sirens conspicuously silent. Mitch felt his heart unraveling.

Del Rey gave them one last look then stepped away to speak with the handful of local policemen who'd responded to calls from the hotel staff.

Mitch, who could feel nothing apart from devastation, managed to find words for his two teammates. "I guess we're leaving."

KATRINA FLOATED UP and away from the nagging pain in her shoulder. As she rose, her consciousness sharpened bringing an awareness of her environment that had been lacking up until then. With astonished curiosity, she realized she was looking down at a small gathering of people—all of them dressed in surgical gowns and masks and standing over a prone body. A plethora of medical instruments whirred and beeped. The patient, lying naked from the waist up, clearly belonged to a female. The patient's hair had been stuffed into a cap, but some of it had escaped, so that a golden-brown tendril spilled over the edge of the operating table, drawing Katrina's notice.

With a sense of shock, she recognized the hair was hers. It occurred to her that she was looking down at her own body, which meant that she was no longer in it.

One of the medical instruments gave a shrill peep.

"She's flat-lining!" announced a nurse in rapid-fire Spanish.

The doctor hissed out a curse. Without pausing in his intent activity—digging into her chest with what looked like tongs—he barked orders for her to be hit with a defibrillator.

Katrina longed to flee the distressing scene. Two

nurses wheeled the defibrillator closer. One snatched up the paddles, placing them on her bare chest.

The other called, "Clear!"

It occurred to Katrina that the choice was hers to stay or go. Sensing a warm light close above her, she was tempted to escape if only to avoid the pain she knew awaited her if she returned. Yet some magnetic pull compelled her to return to her body. A promise. Yes, she was bound by a promise, one she intended to keep.

Mitchell.

His name came suddenly to mind, followed by a powerful rush of emotion. He had said that he would wait for her. She couldn't let him down.

Beep.

With a violent jerk and sudden discomfort, Katrina returned to her flesh.

THE 747 WAS still lumbering toward the arrivals terminal when Mitchell powered on his cell phone. *Halleluiah.* Now that they were back on the east coast, his phone worked. Through eyes that stung from sleep deprivation and ignoring the voice mail from his task unit commander, Mitch accessed the number he'd transferred from del Rey's business card into his contacts.

By now, eight hours after the shooting, del Rey would have definitive news on Katrina's condition.

Over the pounding in his temple that had worsened over the course of the flight, Mitch listened to del Rey's phone ring and ring. When his call went to voicemail, he left a terse message for the captain to return it and apprise him of Katrina's status.

Lowering his arm, he suffered the queasy sensation that something awful had happened to her. Granted, it was probably dinnertime back in Spain, but the man ought to be answering his phone—unless he had bad news he didn't want to share.

Between the headache that was battering his cranium and his reluctance to jump into a time-critical operation, Mitch dragged himself off the plane. He, Chuck, and Austin funneled silently into customs.

As they waited in line to get their passports checked, Mitch regarded his phone in the hopes that he'd overlooked a return call. Nothing.

A sudden thought had him accessing Safari to search for a news story. Surely, the reporters who had descended on El Abanico Hotel would have followed up to discover the fate of the woman shot in the hotel lobby.

He performed a search, plugging in Katrina's full name. With rising amazement, he garnered immediate results—news stories dating to that same day. Opening an article published by *La Vanguardia* entitled "Shooting in Seville tied to Catalan Independence Movement," he waded through the passages in search of Katrina's fate.

A shooting took place at 8 a.m. this morning in El Abanico Hotel in Seville, that resulted in the arrest of Martín José Ferrer, believed to be the mastermind behind Sunday's bombing of La Boquería, Barcelona's largest outdoor market. Ferrer had allegedly traveled to Seville yesterday in pursuit of his half-sister, Katrina Ferrer, who may have betrayed her brother's activities to the Civil Guard. The shooting has been labeled an act of retaliation. The victim, Katrina Ferrer, was shot in the shoulder and taken to Hospital Victoria Eugenia, where she later died...

Mitch's gaze froze on the word *murió*. Shock dumped ice into his bloodstream. A buzzing filled his ears. The customs area became an indistinct blur.

Katrina was dead.

How could that be? He had held her in his arms less than twenty-four hours ago. All that vitality, all that passion, could not be gone—just like that.

Acid seared his throat, warning him of impending disgrace. Without a word to his companions, Mitch bolted for the nearest restroom, arriving in the nick of time to empty the contents of his stomach in a toilet.

CHAPTER FOURTEEN

*I*S THIS THE PLACE?

Stepping from the back seat of the cab she had caught from Norfolk International Airport, Katrina eyed the small cabin nestled under a copse of large trees with a mix of excitement and reservation. It looked different than it had in Mitch's photo, when the oaks had been lush with leaves, the azalea bushes blooming.

Now, in the middle of February, through the vapor of her own breath, the bare branches of the trees struck her as unwelcoming. The cabin's dark windows gave it a desolate air. No doubt it was cold, too, given the absence of smoke coming from the stone chimney—and no electricity either, she reminded herself.

Managing a thank you for the cab driver, who'd gotten out to fetch her suitcase from the trunk, she tipped him and waved him away.

With an indrawn breath, she started for the cabin while feeling in her pocket for the key Mitch had given her. Squeezing it, she let the rough edge cut into her palm to ground herself.

This is finally happening. She had dreamed of this moment for so long, it struck her as unreal. Yet the relief she'd thought she would be feeling remained at bay.

What if Mitch's offer no longer remained? A bed of dry leaves crackled under the soles of her boots as she neared the front stoop. An icy breeze sloughed the tree branches overhead, carrying the scent of wood smoke and drawing a chill up her spine. After all, he had never replied to her email, sent about a week earlier.

Had he even received her explanation for not writing? Her request for shelter?

After all, she'd awakened from her surgery asking for him, only to learn from del Rey that Mitch and his teammates had been summoned home for some untimely mission. For months after that, she'd been placed in witness protection and denied access to the internet, lest someone from her previous life discover her existence. The ruse had been necessary, del Rey had explained, to keep her from facing charges and to protect her from any more attempts on her life. She had explained all that to Mitch in her email.

It wasn't until the trial was underway that she

learned del Rey had spread the rumor she was dead. Her horror had been immediate.

"Everyone believes I'm dead? Mitch, too?" she'd demanded.

"No, no, no." Del Rey had soothed her with the assurance that he'd sent Mitch's commander a certified letter advising them both of Katrina's situation. Mitch would have gotten the letter when he returned from the emergency assignment that had called him away.

But had he?

Sudden doubt brought Katrina to a halt near the cabin's front door. A spider web, abandoned when the weather turned cold, draped from the eves, suggesting the home had not been occupied any time recently. Surely, if Mitch had been expecting her, he'd have cleaned the place up just a bit, not that she expected him to go out of his way for her.

If he *hadn't* known of her arrival, then he must not have gotten her email.

Dear God. Dismay kept her frozen for a minute as a crow, eying her from a branch overhead, cackled at her.

She had no choice but to help herself to Mitch's home. He had offered, she reasoned. After she settled in, got her bearings, and bought a new cell phone under the name del Rey had given her, she would track down Mitch—and give him the shock of his life.

This isn't what I'd hoped for.

The vision she had spun in her mind to get her through their months apart splintered and then crumbled to dust. Four months was a long time. If Mitch had thought her dead all that time, he might well have found another.

HALFWAY DOWN THE driveway to his cabin, Mitch jammed on the brakes. In the next instant, he extinguished his truck's headlights, plunging the woods around his cabin into darkness. The firelight dancing in the hearth inside his supposedly *vacant* home came sharply into focus.

What the hell? Someone was in there. They'd built a fire to keep warm. More than that, they'd lit at least two of his oil lamps in utter disregard for the fact that they were trespassing.

Son of a bitch. Cutting off his engine, Mitch took the time to think through his approach. He was wearing, as he always did, his personal pistol in the paddle holster under his left arm. Unlike the Astra 600 he'd tried using in Spain, the Sig Sauer 226 with the SAS melt had never jammed on him. His trusty folding dagger was still riding in his thigh pocket, where it had been throughout the op he'd just returned from.

Reaching for a couple of the zip-ties he carried in his glove box, he stuffed them into the pocket in the lining of his coat, silenced his cell phone, and made sure the interior light in his truck stayed off when he opened the driver's door. Shutting it quietly behind him, he stepped off the driveway to circle the house.

Exactly how many squatters was he dealing with?

Annoyance tapped at his temples as he peered into the dwelling's interior. The trespassers couldn't have picked a worse time to break into his house. He'd just come off a grueling four-month op in Venezuela. His job had sucked the last ounce of energy from him—though he had to admit that without the distraction, Katrina's death might have sent him into deep depression.

He acknowledged the dark cloud of despair hovering on the fringes of his mind, waiting to ambush him the moment he wasn't in survival mode. In fact, that was the reason he'd gone straight from their debriefing at Spec Ops to his cabin. He'd known he would time alone in which to mourn. Discovering someone had taken advantage of his absence really put his back up.

A lumpy shadow on the wall let him know someone was sitting in his favorite recliner, right in front of the fire. Poor son of a bitch didn't know what was about to hit him.

Mitch listened for voices. Not a sound came

from within. The shadow didn't move, suggesting whoever was in his chair had fallen. His mind flashed to the story of *Goldilocks*.

If only fairytales were real.

Mitch crept toward the back door leading into the tiny house's country kitchen. Feeling under a loose brick, he expected the hidden key to be missing, only to feel its metallic edge. The squatter must have broken in through the front door since the back was still locked.

Letting himself in, he slipped silently into his home. The familiar fragrance of pine and cedar was overlaid by something floral. A sense of surrealism accompanied his stealthy footsteps as he crossed the kitchen, his Sig Sauer at the ready.

Halfway toward the recliner, he froze. Firelight reflected off a tendril of hair resting on the arm of the chair. The delicate features of the woman snoozing against the overstuffed high back wreaked havoc on Mitch's mind. His heart hammered. *I'm dreaming.*

He had dreamed of her so often—exactly like this. His mind had to be playing tricks on him.

Some sound, some movement must have betrayed him—maybe his incredulous gasp of breath—for her eyes floated open.

Sensing the presence of another, Katrina leaped out of the chair.

"Who's there?" she demanded hugging herself as she stared at his dark shape.

He realized she couldn't see him. "It's me. Mitch."

"Mitch?" Throwing her arms open, she flew at him. He had scarcely reset the safety on his gun before she hurtled into his arms.

"Oh, thank God," she cried, gripping him fiercely. "You did get my email."

Stunned by what was clearly real and not a figment of his tortured mind, Mitch hugged her back. Delight and confusion collided, leaving him dazed. He could feel her heat, her curves pressing against him. Warm lips kissed his neck fervently and tracked to his jaw.

"What email?" he asked stupidly, the only thought he could fully process when so many were clamoring through his brain.

His question had her pulling back. Faint firelight illuminated her confusion.

"The one I sent last week. That's why you're here, isn't it?"

He shook his head. "I've been out of the country. I haven't checked my mail in months."

"Oh," she said. "But you're here."

Half-afraid she would vanish on him, he caught her face in his hands, traced the smooth skin of her cheek with his thumb. "And you're alive."

She gasped with what sounded like anger.

"They said you were dead," he continued. "I saw it on the news."

"But del Rey sent a letter to your commander, explaining that was just a ruse."

"Captain Montgomery?" He shook his head. "I haven't seen him in months. I went straight from vacation to four months of hell in South America."

"Oh, my God," Katrina murmured as pity followed quickly on the heels of her wrath. "All this time, you thought me dead?"

"I read it in the news," he repeated, recalling that awful moment at the airport. "You died in the hospital."

"I almost did. That's what gave del Rey the idea to spread the rumor for my benefit—and his," she added on a harder note.

Mitch's smile faded as he recollected the news he'd followed, even though it pained him. "Your brothers went to jail."

"Martí for life," she affirmed. "Jordi got five years."

His thumbs traced her cheekbones. Having stared at her picture on his phone at least a thousand times, every curve, every feature was known to him.

"You're even more beautiful in real life," he asserted.

She searched his expression with a suggestion of

doubt. "I hope…," she started, then faltered. "I hope it's not a problem for me to be here. I understand if you've… moved on or if you've found someone else. I promise I won't—"

"Katrina." He cut her off abruptly, dropping his hands to her shoulders to give her a gentle shake. "Stop. Please." The joy of her resurrection was just beginning to dawn on him. "You're alive! You're fucking alive!" He gripped her harder.

Hope brought a tentative smile to her face. "Do you still love me?"

"Hell, yes," he assured her. Irate feelings edged his joy aside, but only momentarily. "I can't believe del Rey didn't answer my voicemail. I must have left at least a dozen."

"I don't think he understood what we found in each other." Katrina smoothed her hands over his shoulders.

With his emotions careening wildly, Mitch buried his nose in her hair battling the urge to cry. Even with his perilous work keeping him distracted, Katrina's death had taken its toll on him. Yet here she was, very much alive, obliterating his despair and brightening his prospects beyond his wildest dreams.

"My love," he said, nuzzling her cheek.

"My love," she echoed, pulling back to look at him Tears of joy sparkled in her eyes.

"Welcome home," he said gruffly. "How do you

like it so far?"

"It's rustic. And cold. And lonely," she answered truthfully. "But not anymore."

Returning her smile, Mitch marveled at the gift he'd been given. Pleasure flared in him like well-dried tinder.

"Let's start over," he suggested.

With a laugh of absolute agreement, she rolled up on her toes and gently, sweetly crushed her mouth to his.

OTHER BOOKS BY
MARLISS MELTON

ECHO PLATOON SERIES
LOOK AGAIN (Novella #1, permanently free)
DANGER CLOSE
HARD LANDING
FRIENDLY FIRE
NEVER FORGET (short novel)
HOT TARGET

TASKFORCE SERIES
THE PROTECTOR
THE GUARDIAN
THE ENFORCER

NAVY SEAL TEAM 12 SERIES
FORGET ME NOT
IN THE DARK
TIME TO RUN
NEXT TO DIE
CODE OF SILENCE, a novella
TOO FAR GONE
LONG GONE, a novella
SHOW NO FEAR

Made in the USA
Coppell, TX
18 May 2021